"I've waited so long for this," he groaned

Matthew's hands held her thighs against his, the hardness of his flesh leaving Jessica in no doubt that his control had gone completely, that there could only be one outcome to this encounter.

"Jessica?" He raised his head at her silence, frowning as he saw her tears. "It isn't what you want, is it?" he asked huskily.

She bit her bottom lip to hold back the sobs. "I—"

"And it isn't really what I want either. I don't want you as my mistress or to be with me in any transient relationship."

"You don't?" Jessica frowned, puzzled.

"No," he said confidently. "I'm looking for a wife, someone to share my bed full-time. And I want you to be that wife."

CAROLE MORTIMER

is also the author of these

Harlequin Presents

323—TEMPTED BY DESIRE
340—SAVAGE INTERLUDE
352—THE TEMPESTUOUS FLAME
365—DECEIT OF A PAGAN
377—FEAR OF LOVE
383—YESTERDAY'S SCARS
388—ENGAGED TO JARROD STONE
406—BRAND OF POSSESSION
418—THE FLAME OF DESIRE
423—LIVING TOGETHER
430—DEVIL LOVER
437—ICE IN HIS VEINS
443—FIRST LOVE, LAST LOVE
452—SATAN'S MASTER
473—FREEDOM TO LOVE
479—POINT OF NO RETURN
502—ONLY LOVER
510—LOVE'S DUEL
518—BURNING OBSESSION
522—RED ROSE FOR LOVE
531—SHADOWED STRANGER
539—FORGOTTEN LOVER
547—FORBIDDEN SURRENDER
556—ELUSIVE LOVER
564—PASSION FROM THE PAST
571—PERFECT PARTNER
579—GOLDEN FEVER
587—HIDDEN LOVE
594—LOVE'S ONLY DECEPTION

Many of these books are available at your local bookseller.

For a free catalog listing all titles currently available,
send your name and address to:

HARLEQUIN READER SERVICE
1440 South Priest Drive, Tempe, AZ 85281
Canadian address: Stratford, Ontario N5A 6W2

CAROLE MORTIMER

captive loving

Harlequin Books

TORONTO • NEW YORK • LOS ANGELES • LONDON
AMSTERDAM • PARIS • SYDNEY • HAMBURG
STOCKHOLM • ATHENS • TOKYO • MILAN

For
John and Matthew

Harlequin Presents first edition June 1983
ISBN 0-373-10603-3

Original hardcover edition published in 1983
by Mills & Boon Limited

Printed in U.S.A.

CHAPTER ONE

THE arms of her young daughter strained about Jessica's neck, and she looked down at her affectionately. Corn-coloured hair, thick and straight like her own, pansy-blue eyes staring into other pansy-blue eyes, the small snub nose and wide smiling mouth all adding up to an almost mirror image. Except that there were twenty years' difference in their ages, Penny was only five years old.

'Do you have to go out, Mummy?' Penny pouted beguilingly. 'I don't want old Aunty Peg taking care of me.'

'She isn't old, darling,' Jessica chuckled, tweaking her daughter's nose. Peg Seabrook was in her early forties, and certainly wouldn't appreciate being described as 'old'. And she knew her daughter's bad humour to be due to anger with her rather than dislike of Peg. Usually Penny and Peg got on well together, and she knew that once she and Andrew had left they would do so again. 'And yes, I have to go out.' She smoothed Penny's hair back from her scrupulously clean face; the bathtime of an hour ago had been as hiliarious as usual.

Penny frowned petulantly. 'But you don't usually go out with Daddy.'

Jessica's face became shadowed. What was the saying 'out of the mouths of babes . . .'? Penny was right, she didn't usually go out with Andrew, but then the way he spent his evenings didn't usually include a wife. She hadn't realised that Penny had been aware of her parents' differing social activities – no, not parents', because she personally didn't have a social life. Andrew had enough for both of them.

'Tonight's special, poppet.' She stood up to tuck the sheets more firmly about her daughter. 'It has to do with Daddy's work.'

Penny looked up at her consideringly. 'Will Aunt Lisa be there too?'

Jessica stiffened, forcing herself to continue tidying the gold-coloured coverlet. 'Aunt Lisa?' she asked with as much casualness as she could summon up.

Her young daughter wrinkled her nose up with dislike. 'She came out with Daddy and me last week when we went shopping for your birthday present,' she revealed innocently, seeing nothing unusual in her father going shopping with another woman.

Damn Andrew! Jessica didn't need two guesses who 'Aunt Lisa' was, she would be the latest in the long line of women Andrew had had since their marriage seven years ago. But he had no right introducing his women to their daughter. Penny was the only good thing to come out of this disaster of a marriage, and she wouldn't have her own relationship with her spoilt by Andrew's carelessness.

The fact that the other woman had probably helped Andrew choose the expensive bottle of perfume he gave her for her birthday didn't even touch her. Nothing Andrew did bothered her any more; it had ceased to very soon after Penny was born. But she would have to talk to him about involving Penny in his sordidness. The thought didn't please her. Andrew had been more unpleasant than usual the last few weeks, and she dreaded him flying into one of his uncontrollable tempers.

'She could be,' she answered Penny evasively, not sure how Andrew had met this woman Lisa. She never knew where he met any of them, she just knew *when* he had met them. After seven years she was an expert at telling the signs, the way he suddenly started spoiling

Penny and ignoring her. Not that she minded the latter part of it, but the sporadic gift-buying and time spent with Penny only confused her when it came to an abrupt end. Jessica would say that this latest affair had been going on a little over two months.

Penny pulled a face. 'I didn't like her.'

'Never mind, darling,' she soothed. 'Perhaps you won't see her again.'

'I hope not.'

'Sleep now, Penny,' Jessica told her firmly. 'And don't play up Aunty Peg, you know she can't resist you.'

The little girl grinned, looking completely angelic with her golden hair spread out on the pillow beneath her, her blue eyes clear and untroubled.

' 'Night,' Jessica laughed, estimating Penny joining Peg downstairs ten minutes after she and Andrew had departed.

' 'Night,' Penny echoed. 'You look lovely, Mummy.'

'Thank you, darling.' There was a catch in her voice. It was so long since she had received a compliment, a compliment of any sort, that tears came unbidden to her eyes.

Damn! She had been all ready to go, and now she would have to recheck her make-up. If she were late Andrew wouldn't be pleased. This company dinner meant a lot to him. He would be downstairs charming Peg at the moment, despite the other woman's seventeen years' seniority. Andrew couldn't be in the same room as a woman and not try and win her over. It had been this same easy charm that had attracted Jessica to him in the first place, the same charm that all his other women found so fascinating, the same charm that had destroyed them.

She went back to her bedroom, the room she had slept in alone since Penny had been three months old.

Andrew's room was next door, but more often than not it was unoccupied during the night hours; his stumblings into the house during the early hours of the morning were a regular thing, although with this latest affair he usually only just managed to get in before Penny got up to go to school.

Jessica studied her reflection in the mirror. Mm, not bad. Andrew had insisted on giving her money for a new dress, and the royal blue crushed velvet of the gown made her eyes appear an even deeper blue, her hair almost silver. She looked cool and confident, and she only hoped she could act that way. Andrew had worked for Sinclairs for two years now, in the Sales Department, but this year was the first time he had invited her to attend one of their annual summer dances. The previous year she had stayed at home to look after an ailing Penny, and Andrew had gone on his own. She doubted he had left the same way. Andrew attracted women like bees around honey, his dark good looks and teasing blue eyes being attractive to most women, his air of recklessness adding to his challenge.

He stood up as soon as she entered the lounge, and she could view dispassionately the way the navy blue suit emphasised the breadth of his shoulders, his tapered waist and muscled thighs. His dark hair was worn over-long, deliberately so, and his features were so perfect he was almost beautiful.

'We'd better be going,' he said tersely, moving his car keys impatiently from one hand to the other, looking older than his twenty-seven years.

'You look wonderful, Jessica.' Peg filled Andrew's omission. 'Really lovely, doesn't she, Andrew?' Her voice hardened over the last.

Jessica bit her lip. Peg wasn't fooled by Andrew's winning ways in the least. She had been their next-door neighbour for two years now, and she knew exactly what Andrew was like. In fact, Peg was always advising her to leave him, if only to teach him a lesson. Peg seemed convinced that this was the jolt Andrew needed to stop his affairs. There was no possibility of her ever leaving Andrew, not with what he knew about her.

Andrew gave her a cursory glance, more of a glower really. 'Yes,' he snapped. 'Now are you ready?'

'I just have to get my jacket——'

'I'll get it.' He strode off impatiently, scowling heavily.

Peg raised her eyebrows; she was an attractive brunette with twelve years of happy marriage behind her, and was obviously slightly bewildered by Jessica's own marriage. 'Big night?' she teased.

'Andrew's just tense,' Jessica excused his rudeness. 'Getting on at Sinclairs means a lot to him. The Sales Manager is retiring at the end of the year, and Andrew would like his job.'

'Isn't he a little young for that?'

She shrugged. 'I suppose he could be, I don't really know.' Andrew rarely discussed his work with her, in fact she felt sure he had only mentioned the Sales Manager's job to her because he wanted to be sure she made a good impression tonight. 'He seems to think he can do it.'

'Then he probably can,' her friend laughed. 'That young man can do anything he sets his mind to.'

Not quite anything, but she wasn't going to tell Peg that. The explanation would be too embarrassing to herself. 'If Penny should come down——'

'She will, you know she will,' Peg chuckled.

'Yes,' Jessica smiled. 'Well, I shouldn't worry about it too much. It's Friday, so she doesn't have school tomorrow.'

'Whatever you say,' the other woman accepted. 'I'll be glad to have her company.'

'Here,' Andrew came back, handing Jessica's jacket to her. 'Let's go,' and he walked out to the car.

'See you later,' she told Peg breathlessly as she struggled into her jacket, hastily following Andrew.

He was already seated behind the wheel, having no intention of opening the car door for her. Jessica saw something glittering on the floor as she got in, and bent to pick it up. It was a woman's compact, and it looked expensive.

'Lisa's?' She held it up.

Andrew turned to her with a start, his attention momentarily diverted from his driving. 'What did you say?'

She drew in a steadying breath, knowing it would do no good for her to lose her temper. 'I wondered if this were Lisa's.'

His face darkened. 'How the hell did you find out about her?'

'Guess,' she said bitterly.

'Penny!'

'Yes. Andrew, I won't have her involved in your affairs. If you want to——'

'*You* won't have her involved?' he repeated scornfully. 'Who asked for your opinion?'

'Can't you see that she'll very soon start to make the connection——'

'So what if she does?'

She paled. 'Andrew, you can't——'

'Who says I can't?' he scowled. 'Who's going to stop me? You?'

Jessica flinched at the contempt in his voice. 'I won't have her involved,' she repeated firmly. 'You won't take her out with one of your women again.'

An angry flush coloured his cheeks, a pulse beating erratically in his cheek. 'And what are you going to do if

I do? Deny me the pleasure of your bed?' he mocked bitterly.

Jessica paled even more. She should be used to his insults by now, and yet she could still be hurt by them. And he knew it, deriving great pleasure from denting the shell she had built up about her emotions.

'But then it never was a pleasure, for either of us, was it?' he added scathingly.

'Andrew——'

'Beautiful—and frigid,' he continued sneeringly.

'I'm not——'

'When a woman hasn't slept with her husband, or had the inclination to, for over five years then there has to be something wrong with her. And don't try and put the blame on me again,' he snapped. 'None of the other women I've slept with have had the trouble you did.'

By 'trouble' she knew he meant inhibitions. When they had met eight years ago she had been so shy it had taken all her time to talk to him, overwhelmed as she was by the fact that such a handsome, popular boy should have been interested in her.

Brought up by a maiden aunt since she was five years old, she wasn't used to being the centre of attention, especially male attention. She had been happy with her parents until the car crash had taken them from her, and her aunt had been very strict, hadn't liked her talking to boys, not even at school, drumming into Jessica at an early age the infidelities of men.

Thinking about it now, in her own maturity, she thought her aunt had probably been very hurt by a man when she was younger, but that didn't excuse the way she had regimentally brought up Jessica, never showing her any love or affection, something that had come hard to her after the first happy five years of her life.

Consequently she had grown up a lonely child, with a craving to be loved that at the time she hadn't even recognised. In her last year of school she had taken a Saturday job working in a local café, much to her aunt's disgust. Andrew came in there a lot with his friends, or with a girl. He had been popular even then, and had seemed like a god to the awe-struck, lovesick Jessica.

When he had asked her out for the first time she had thought he hadn't really meant it, that he had done it as a joke, that he and his friends would have a laugh about it later. Her basic insecurity was such that she hadn't been able to acknowledge or recognise her own beauty—she still couldn't, but Andrew had been intrigued by that haunting beauty from the first.

He had started to come to the café alone after that, asking her out again and again, until she finally agreed to let him take her to the cinema, little guessing that he had taken her first refusals as simply playing hard to get. When he had kissed her in the back row of the cinema she had let him, feeling safe in amongst all those people. But when he tried to do the same thing outside her aunt's house she had shrugged off his advances.

That had been the start of a long, slow courtship, with Jessica believing she had at last found the love and tenderness she craved. She had learnt later that Andrew's thoughts were less emotional, more basic. She parried his more intimate caresses with a shyness she later learnt he thought to be an act.

By this time it had become a challenge to him to possess her, almost an obsession, and when her aunt had died suddenly just after Jessica's eighteenth birthday he had even married her to realise his obsession. Their wedding night had been a triumph for him, and a deep shock for her. She had thought that because she loved him he would be tender and understanding about her inexperience, would respect her virginity. But he had been brutal, and his lovemaking contained only self-gratification, leaving her bruised and hurting, and worst of all, humiliated.

But she had been too inexperienced, too ignorant, to realise that there was more to going to bed with a man than what Andrew gave her, and lay docilely beneath him while he satisfied himself with her.

For months she had continued to suffer his invasion of her body, knowing that he enjoyed subjugating her. But by this time she had a job of her own, a job where the intimacies of married life were discussed between the women quite openly, and being one of the married ones herself she was expected to know what they were talking about. She didn't. But it was from these women that she had began to wonder if she wasn't missing something, if perhaps there *wasn't* more to making love.

When she had dared to broach the subject to Andrew he had exploded in a storm of anger so fierce he had frightened her. He had taken her words as a personal attack on his manhood, had told her that her lack of pleasure was due to her own frigidness, that it had nothing to do with him, that all the other women he slept with enjoyed it as much as he did, that none of them had her prudish inhibitions.

It was the first she had known of his other women, and her humiliation had been extreme as she found there had been other women in his life almost from the day they had been married. She had been numbed by the revelation, although she had stayed with him, still loving him, and having nowhere else to go even if she did leave.

A few months later she had found out she was pregnant, and so there had been no question of leaving Andrew then. But shortly after that pregnancy the physical side of their marriage had been permanently terminated, at her instigation, and Andrew had never let her forget it. Every time they had an argument he brought the subject up, always accusing, always threatening. And she feared those threats.

'I'm sorry, Andrew,' she said quietly now. 'But after Penny was born——'

'It had nothing to do with that, and you know it,' he scorned. 'You were always frigid, right from the start. I should have divorced you long ago.'

'Oh no!' she cried her dismay, her face very white. 'You wouldn't, would you, Andrew?' She clutched on to his arm.

'Don't do that when I'm driving,' he shook off her hand angrily. 'In fact, don't do it at all, you know I can't bear you to touch me.'

Jessica recoiled back to her own side of the car, looking down at her hands as they moved nervously in her lap. She stopped their convulsive movement, clenching them tightly together. 'I'm sorry, Andrew,' she said huskily.

'So I should damn well think,' he snapped. 'Just who do you think you are to tell me how to behave with my own daughter?'

She could have said his wife, but she knew what his answer to that would be. Besides, she daren't antagonise him too much, not when he could ultimately use the threat of divorce, a threat which he knew would cow her once and for all.

She forced her voice to be controlled, reasoning. 'I just don't think it's a good idea for Penny to meet—your friend Lisa,' she chose her words carefully.

'Her name is Alicia, actually,' he drawled. 'Only her—intimates, call her Lisa.'

'Oh.'

'And I think it's a very good idea for Penny to meet her, she could be her stepmother one day,' he added tauntingly.

Jessica's breath caught in her throat. 'Is——is that probable?'

He shrugged. 'Anything is possible.' He made no effort to reassure her.

'Andrew——'

'Jessica!' he mocked, turning the low sports car into the car park of the Sinclair office building.

'Are you——' she swallowed hard, licking her lips nervously, 'are you thinking of divorcing me?'

He swung out of the car, bending down to speak to her. 'It's never far from my mind,' he told her cruelly. 'It's no picnic being married to a silent iceberg.'

'I——'

'Don't make the same grand offer to share my bed again,' he said sneeringly. 'I wouldn't have you as a gift. I like co-operation in my bed, not complacency.'

Sharing a bed with Andrew had been the last thing on her mind, although she knew she would do even that if it would stop him talking of divorce. Thank goodness she no longer held any attraction for him!

'I just wanted to say——'

'It can wait until later, Jessica,' he dismissed impatiently. 'Right now I want to go in there and make an impression on Sinclair. And you're going to help me. A beautiful wife is always an asset.' He took hold of her elbow as she joined him on the tarmacked car park, his mouth twisting mockingly. 'Only I will know that the provocation in those pansy-blue eyes of yours is just a façade, a lie.'

Jessica ignored his jibe, having already taken too much of a battering for one evening. 'Will Lis—— Alicia be there?' she persisted as they entered the ultra-modern building with several other couples, who Andrew greeted as they all stepped into the lift together, making no effort to introduce her.

'Of course,' Andrew muttered tersely, not even looking down at her. 'She's Sinclair's secretary. Always go to the top, I say,' he added crudely.

Jessica felt ill, recoiling as they stepped out on to the eighth floor, the noise from the party already under way filling her with dread. She never appeared well at these sort of functions, her basic shyness holding her back from joining in the merriment, although sometimes she wished this weren't so, wished she could be the sort of woman that men were attracted to.

'I have to go to the powder-room,' she told Andrew in a whisper.

He sighed heavily. 'Down the corridor,' he instructed curtly. 'Second door on the left.' He turned in the direction of the party.

'Andrew!' she called in a panicked voice, already self-conscious as several of Andrew's work colleagues stared at her curiously. No doubt every single one of them knew of his affairs, especially this latest one with the boss's secretary. Andrew liked to boast of his conquests.

'Yes?' His patience, what there was of it, was wearing very thin.

'I——My jacket,' she said lamely.

He wasn't exactly gentle as he helped her off with it. 'And don't be long,' he ordered.

'You'll wait for me?' she asked anxiously.

'I'll meet you inside.'

Jessica looked into the darkened room, the noise from the live music and chattering people suddenly seeming louder to her. 'But I won't be able to find you in there,' she said in dismay.

'Then I'll find you,' he dismissed. 'And for heaven's sake hurry up, Jessica. I want to introduce you to Sinclair.'

There was no point in arguing further, Andrew would only do what he wanted to do in the end, so she made her way down the badly lit corridor, blinking back her tears. She was so tearful tonight! Andrew had said much worse things to her in the past and she hadn't even flinched. But tonight she was feeling particularly vulnerable, especially with Andrew's mention of divorce. Could he really be serious about Alicia?

She knew almost immediately that she had entered the wrong room, the overhead florescent lighting showing this to be an office, the teak desk cleared of all work, the swivel-chair behind the desk turned towards the window. The view of the surrounding countryside had a beauty of its own from this height, and she spent a minute or so drinking in the peace and tranquillity, finally turning to go in search of the powder-room.

'Don't go.'

Jessica froze, slowly turning in the direction of that silky voice. The swivel-chair had been spun round to reveal a man, a ruggedly handsome man who was looking at her with open admiration, a man of perhaps thirty-five or thirty-six.

Tawny eyes were narrowed appreciatively, the hair a deep burnished gold, worn rather long, his skin deeply tanned, as if he had recently been on holiday. Beneath the tawny eyes the nose jutted out slightly aquiline, his mouth curved into a smile, sensually so. As he stood up, easily over six feet, a good foot taller than her own meagre height, Jessica could see how well the white dinner jacket fitted across his powerful shoulders, tapering to a narrow waist, and muscular thighs clearly outlined in the black tailored trousers he wore. He was tall, and powerful, and he made her feel uneasy.

The way he was looking at her now made her blush, every inch of her having known the fire of his gaze. 'I——I'm sorry,' she stuttered. 'I was looking for—I came in the wrong door.' Hot colour flooded her cheeks.

His smile deepened to humour, his teeth very white against his tan. 'The ladies' room is next door,' he drawled.

'Er——yes.' She turned to go.

'Stay,' he repeated his earlier request.

Her lids flickered up in surprise, her lashes long and dark, tipped with gold. 'The dance . . .'

'Can get along without us very well for a few minutes.' He took her arm, steering her over to the swivel-chair he had just vacated. 'I wonder who you belong to,' he muttered almost to himself.

'I don't belong to anyone,' Jessica surprised herself by snapping at him.

'Good,' he smiled. 'Because I think I'd like you to belong to me.'

She struggled to get out of the chair, but found her way blocked by his powerful frame as he sat on the desk in front of her, his legs either side of her stopping her turning the chair.

'Will you let me go, Mr——'

'Matthew,' he murmured softly, gently touching the silver of her hair. 'Just Matthew.'

She squirmed away from him. 'Don't do that!' Two spots of angry colour darkened her cheeks.

'Why not?' His hand didn't move away from her, caressing her cheek now. 'Your name—what's your name?' he demanded impatiently.

'Jessica. But——'

'Not Jess? I hope not, because I don't like names to be abbreviated.' He made this comment as if he expected his likes and dislikes to matter to her.

Well, they didn't And neither did he. 'If you'll excuse me . . .' She tried to brush past him, but he wouldn't let her go.

'I can't do that, Jessica,' he said the name with enjoyment, savouring every syllable. 'Mm, it suits you. My lovely Jessica.' His tawny eyes held her captive. 'I was sitting in that chair wondering how I was going to get through the evening when I looked up and saw your reflection in the window. Do you have any idea how lovely you are?'

'If you're the office Romeo——'

'Oh, not me, Jessica,' he smiled, his hands on the arm of the chair pinning her back against the leather. 'That's Baxter's prerogative.'

Andrew! Everyone did know about his affairs, including this man! The two of them could even work together, and this man Matthew would probably enjoy telling Andrew how he had frightened his wife half to death. Andrew would never forgive her if this man should even guess at their sterile relationship.

'I've heard he's a flirt,' she said lightly, doing her best not to panic. She would just sit this out, he was bound to tire of teasing her soon.

'He is. But I don't want to talk about him,' Matthew dismissed. 'Will you promise the rest of the evening to me?'

Jessica gasped. 'Of course not!'

'You have to!' His hands gripped hers, his expression intent. 'Jessica, I'd just about given up on you.'

'But I've never met you before!'

'If you had I wouldn't have been feeling so despondent about this dance. I hate Company dances,' he grimaced.

'So do I.'

'You see?' he said eagerly. 'We have a lot in common.'

'Mr—Matthew, disliking Company dances means we have one thing in common,' Jessica pointed out mockingly, pleased with herself for her calm. This man could just be flirting with her, or he could be slightly unbalanced, whatever he was he was dangerous; there was a predatory light in the tawny eyes.

'We're attracted to each other,' he claimed arrogantly.

'We most certainly are not!' she gasped, wondering at his raw audacity. Andrew might be a womaniser, but this man easily beat him!

'But we are, Jessica. I've been waiting all my life for you——'

'Isn't that approach a little hackneyed?' She scorned to hide her rising panic. He didn't seem to be tiring of this game at all, in fact he seemed to be getting bolder, his thumbs sensually caressing the back of her hands, desire in his eyes.

Heavens, she was so alone with him here, and Andrew or no Andrew, she was going to scream in a minute!

The man frowned darkly. 'It isn't hackneyed if it's the truth,' he rasped.

She looked at him steadily, forcing herself to do so. 'It may be true for you, but it certainly isn't true for me.'

'Of course it is,' he dismissed impatiently. 'I refuse to believe——'

'And I refuse to listen to this—rubbish any more,' she cut in coldly. 'I'm sure this approach has worked for you in the past, but I'm afraid that this time you've struck out. Perhaps you ought to take lessons from Andrew Baxter,' she added bitterly.

'Jessica——'

'Would you please get out of my way.' She looked up at him with cold eyes. 'I'd like to get back to the party,' she lied.

'I'm not losing you now I've found you,' Matthew told her firmly. 'Will you come and dance with me?'

She knew it was just an excuse for him to get her into his arms, could see that in the naked desire in his eyes, but it could also be a way for her to get out of here. 'I have to go to the ladies' room first,' she reminded him huskily.

'Do you have any idea how sexy your voice is?' he asked deeply.

Did nothing stop this man? He probably had a wife waiting for him in the other room! She pitied her even as she pitied herself. Maybe the two of them should get together and trade unfaithful husband stories!

'Jessica,' Matthew prompted her attention back to him. 'Why do I get the impression you keep fading off from me?' he frowned.

Maybe be cause she did! She had become so used to shutting herself off from Andrew that she often did it without even realising it. And this man's flirting turned her off more than anything, despite his undoubted attraction. She was married to a man who was too good-looking for his own good, and this man was just an older version of Andrew.

She gave him a bright meaningless smile. 'You were just telling me how sexy my voice is,' she recited to show she had been listening, another habit she had picked up from being married to Andrew.

Matthew smiled. 'Very sexy,' he confirmed throatily. 'It's deep and husky, with a slight catch in it that sends shivers down my spine.'

He had certainly noticed a lot about her in these few brief minutes of conversation! 'I'm glad you like it,' she said lightly, wondering when he was going to let her go. Andrew would be getting impatient, and if he became angry with her there was no telling what would happen.

'I more than like it,' he said huskily, his face dangerously close to hers. 'Jessica——'

'I really do have to go to the ladies' room,' she interrupted jerkily, knowing that if he got any closer to her she was going to make a fool of herself.

'All right,' Matthew moved back with a sigh. 'But you'll give me that dance?'

She would promise him anything to get out of here.

'If that's what you want,' she nodded.

'It isn't—but I'll settle for that. For now.'

He at last allowed her to stand up, and she moved quickly to the door. 'I'll meet you inside,' she told him, knowing she intended doing no such thing.

Matthew obviously knew it too. 'I'll wait in the corridor for you,' he made the answer Andrew should have made a few minutes ago.

'All right.' Jessica's tone was agitated. 'I'll meet you outside the dance-room.' Maybe she could avoid him in the crowd.

'I'll wait for you outside here.' He foiled that plan too.

She gave an impatient sigh, leaving by the door he opened for her, entering the room next door with a sense of relief.

Maybe if she stayed here long enough he would tire of waiting and go back to the party, although the determination in those tawny eyes hadn't given any indication of that. Matthew appeared to be a man who liked his own way, his arrogance was a fundamental part of his personality.

She hadn't realised she had noticed so much about him! She rarely noticed men at all, being shyly polite to the few male acquaintances Andrew had introduced her to in the past, and yet Matthew hadn't made it possible for her to behave either shyly or politely. He really was the most arrogant man!

But she couldn't sit here all night. She had left Andrew over fifteen minutes ago, and if she didn't soon return he was likely to come looking for her. Maybe Matthew would have returned to his wife by now.

No such luck. He was leaning back lazily against the wall when she stepped out into the corridor, his hands thrust casually into his trousers pockets, although he seemed to sense her presence immediately, straightening away from the wall, his eyes darkening appreciatively as he slowly studied her from the top of her gleaming head to the tips of her tiny feet.

He came forward to grasp her elbow, his hold possessive. 'I wasn't sure I hadn't dreamt you,' he murmured throatily, his gaze warm on her flushed face.

'It's rather early in the evening to be drunk,' Jessica said coldly.

'I'm not drunk,' he smiled. 'At least, not from alcohol. I had an awful feeling you might try and slip away from me.'

She allowed herself to be steered in the direction of the room where the loud music and noisy chatter seemed to have risen to a crescendo, feeling relief that at least she wasn't to be alone when she went in there, although she would rather it hadn't been this man at her side.

Consequently her voice was sharp when next she spoke. 'There was no way I could do that,' she snapped.

'I'm glad,' he squeezed her elbow. 'I don't want to lose you now I've found you.'

As soon as she found Andrew she would make sure she never spoke to this maniac again!

But Andrew was nowhere to be seen, not at the bar, and not on the dance floor. Her imagination told her only too accurately what he was probably doing—and it wouldn't be anything innocent, not if his latest mistress were here.

He could have behaved himself one evening, especially in front of his boss. She was sure it wasn't going to impress John Sinclair to see Andrew flirting with his own secretary!

'You seem to be looking for someone,' Matthew remarked deeply at her side.

'I am,' she snapped her resentment that he was still

there. So far the evening was turning out to be a complete disaster.

'The man you came with?' he said shrewdly.

'My husband, yes,' she nodded, watching as he seemed to pale at her disclosure.

'Your husband . . .?' he repeated softly. 'He's here?' His hand dropped away from her elbow.

'Oh yes,' she gave a bitter smile.

'Where?' Matthew rasped.

Her eyes flashed deeply blue. 'If I knew that I wouldn't be looking for him.'

He seemed rather dazed. 'It never occurred to me that you were married . . . Have you been married long?' he asked harshly.

'Seven years,' she supplied tightly. Andrew was still nowhere in sight.

He groaned, very pale, his eyes the yellow of a cat's. 'Children?'

'One,' Jessica nodded. 'A little girl.'

He put a hand up to his brow, all teasing gone now. 'I—You didn't tell me you were married!'

'You didn't ask.' She had at last spotted Andrew. He was coming towards them, and fortunately he didn't look angry at all, smiling his most charming smile as his arm slipped about her waist.

'Here you are, darling,' he said in a softly chiding voice. 'I've been looking everywhere for you.'

By the smell of his breath he had done most of his looking at the bar! 'I've been looking for you too, darling.' The last was added for the benefit of the man called Matthew, letting him know once and for all to leave her alone.

'Your wife has been in safe hands, Baxter,' he remarked tautly, his mouth twisting as he looked at Andrew.

'Jessica hasn't been bothering you, sir?' Andrew

asked anxiously, all his earlier contempt gone from his voice.

Sir? Jessica stiffened. This man must be one of Andrew's bosses! She hadn't said anything that could have upset him, had she?

'Not at all,' Matthew replied easily, his eyes narrowed. 'Although we haven't really had the opportunity to introduce ourselves properly.' He looked expectantly at Andrew.

'My wife Jessica,' he instantly introduced. 'Jessica, this is Matthew Sinclair, the owner of Sinclairs.'

Not just one of Andrew's bosses—*the* boss!

CHAPTER TWO

SHE should have known, should have guessed by Andrew's charming manner just now, that the man she knew simply as Matthew was someone important. No, not just someone important, he was the man Andrew most wanted to impress. And he had been flirting with her shamelessly.

She looked up at Andrew. 'I thought that was John Sinclair?'

It was Matthew who answered her. 'I am John Sinclair, but so was my father. I prefer to use my second name rather than be called Young John Sinclair.' His mouth twisted derisively.

Jessica looked at him with new eyes, no longer seeing the man who had tried to pick her up a few minutes ago, now seeing the authority that was second nature to him, his autocratic bearing. He was everything the wealthy owner of Sinclair's should be, Sinclair Office Supplies having tentacles all over the world, and she should have seen that in him from the first.

'Your wife had just promised me a dance,' he told Andrew. 'That is, if you have no objection,' he added as an afterthought.

'No, of course not,' Andrew answered, as Jessica had known he would, flushing his pleasure that Matthew Sinclair had chosen his wife out of all the other females in the room; most of them were just waiting for the owner of the firm to notice them.

'Jessica?' Matthew Sinclair quirked a questioning eyebrow at her.

'I——' She broke off her refusal as Andrew's fingers

bit painfully into her waist. 'I would love to,' she amended, knowing she would never hear the end of it if she turned this man down. Andrew would surely never forgive her. And those threats of divorce earlier had sounded genuine enough.

They were the cynosure of all eyes as they stepped on to the dance floor, the fast disco-sound giving way to a slow love song, couples moving naturally into each other's arms as they swayed together to the music.

'I couldn't have chosen better myself,' Matthew murmured as the theme from *Love Story* became audible. He slowly pulled her into his arms, making no effort to hold her formally, as one would have expected between employer and employee's wife, his hands resting possessively on her hips as his body moved sensually against hers, his temple resting lightly against hers.

Jessica at once felt panic, and pushed at his shoulders. 'Please—don't do that,' she said awkwardly, feeling his tension even in her inexperience.

Matthew looked down at her with puzzled eyes, dancing slightly away from her now. 'You must have been very young when you married,' he said gruffly.

She nodded, not looking at him. 'Eighteen.'

'Do you love him?'

Her lashes fluttered nervously, and she looked hastily away from probing tawny eyes. 'Of course I love him,' she answered sharply, too sharply, realising how defensive she sounded. 'Andrew is my husband,' she added simply.

'For better, for worse?' Matthew scorned tightly.

'Exactly.'

'Jessica——'

'I think the music has stopped, Mr Sinclair.' She moved away from him.

He made no effort to leave the dance floor, attracting

several curious looks. 'You want me to take you back to Andrew?' he asked huskily.

She knew there was much more significance behind the words than appeared on the surface. And this had to stop now. Not even for Andrew and the sake of his promotion would she put up with this man's familiarity.

'Yes, I would,' she replied stiltedly. 'And isn't it time you returned to your wife?'

'I don't have a wife, Jessica,' he told her deeply. 'Unlike you, I was patient.'

'Patient . . .?' She shook her head. 'I'm sorry, I don't know what you mean.'

'No,' he sighed, 'I can see you don't. And I'm not in a position to tell you, not any more. Come on, I'll take you back to your husband.'

'Thank you,' she nodded coolly.

Matthew's hand on her elbow was impersonal as he guided her back to Andrew's side. 'Maybe I could borrow your wife for another dance later?' he said with stilted politeness.

'Of course, sir,' Andrew agreed eagerly, without even consulting her. 'Jessica would like that,' he added enthusiastically.

'Jessica,' Matthew nodded abruptly before leaving them.

Andrew dragged her over to a vacant table near the bar. 'I don't know how you did it,' he said excitedly, 'but you certainly made a hit with Sinclair!'

'Don't be silly, Andrew.' She looked away, blushing unconsciously, noting that Matthew Sinclair was now dancing with a tall black-haired woman, her voluptuous figure shown to advantage in the green gown she wore, the two of them dancing even closer together than he and Jessica had. She turned back to Andrew. 'I merely met him outside—in the corridor.' She didn't want to tell him she had gone into the wrong room, he would only berate her for her stupidity. 'He—he offered to escort me in here.'

'He likes you,' Andrew insisted. 'Sinclair has always seemed a very cold fish to me. But he certainly didn't act that way with you.'

No, he certainly hadn't, although she thought she had got her feelings of uninterest over to him now. 'He isn't acting that way with his partner now either,' she pointed out dryly.

Andrew looked towards the dance-floor, easily locating Matthew Sinclair and his partner. 'Don't be ridiculous, Jessica—that's Lisa,' he scowled.

Jessica's eyes widened as she looked at the other woman with new eyes. Yes, she would be the sort of woman who appealed to Andrew, her sexuality oozed from every pore in her body.

And it was just like Andrew to be jealous of Matthew Sinclair's attention to his mistress, and consider the same attention shown to his wife an asset!

Lisa—or Alicia, to give her her real name—was strikingly beautiful, in her early twenties, with a figure any model would envy, except perhaps that her bust was a little too full to suit their slenderness. And she certainly didn't look as if she minded having Matthew Sinclair's arms about her; her own arms were entwined about his neck as they moved slowly in time to the music.

Andrew was scowling heavily now, his anger deepening as Matthew Sinclair and Alicia went to the bar together once the music had stopped. 'Excuse me,' he mumbled, and stood up, making his own way to the bar. After buying himself a drink he sauntered over to join the other couple.

Jessica turned away to hide her shame. He was making himself so obvious, making a fool of himself.

'Hello there, love,' greeted a cheery voice. 'All alone, are you?'

She looked up into the face of a man who had obviously had too much to drink already, a man in his forties, very overweight, an alcoholic flush to his flabby cheeks. And he seemed to have singled her out for his inebriated attention. 'No, I'm not alone,' she told him in her coldest voice. 'My partner will be back in a moment,' although by the look of Andrew he wasn't going to leave Alicia's side for some time to come, and Matthew Sinclair was noticeably absent from their group now.

'Not if he's Andrew Baxter, he won't.' The drunken man pulled out a chair and sat down. 'Randy Andy, we call him in the office.' He gave a suggestive laugh, his expression leering. 'That's because he is.' The man leant forward over the table, breathing beer fumes all over her. 'Randy, I mean.'

Jessica had stiffened at his insulting tone. 'The—nickname you have for Andrew is of no interest to me.' She stood up. 'If you'll excuse me . . .' She had no idea where she was going, just away from this man.

'Hey, not so fast!' His hand came out and caught her about the wrist, surprisingly strong. 'If you don't want to talk about Rand—er—Andy, then we won't. I can understand you being annoyed with him, he shouldn't really have bothered to bring one of his little friends when he already has Alicia,' he chuckled. 'You can be my little friend if you like.'

The idea nauseated her. '*Andy* brought his wife with him this time,' she snapped. 'Now, would you take your hands off me?'

He let go of her as if she had burnt him. 'Cold little bitch, aren't you?' he glared his dislike. 'No wonder Andy says you're frigid! You should give the man what he wants——'

Jessica didn't wait to hear any more, but turned to

rush out of the room, her face deathly white. Andrew had talked about her to that man, had discussed their sexual differences with a total stranger. She could just imagine the crudeness of that conversation, the ribald remarks! Did everyone in that room know she didn't sleep with her husband?

'Jessica!'

She stopped her mad flight at the sound of that familiar voice, and turned to find Matthew Sinclair striding down the corridor to join her.

He grasped her forearms, searching her pale features. 'Jessica, are you all right? Did Taylor insult you?' he demanded in an angry voice.

'Taylor?' she echoed dully. Did this man know of her marital difficulties too? If he did then Andrew bringing her here tonight was a waste of time.

'The man you were talking to——'

'I wasn't talking to him, he was talking to me.' She blinked back the tears.

'Jessica . . .' Matthew groaned.

'Please, let me go.' She shook off his hands, regaining her composure with effort. 'Mr Taylor didn't insult me, he—he's just a little drunk, I think.'

Matthew nodded grimly. 'More than a little. I'll get someone to take him home.'

Jessica would have liked to go home too, but Andrew had disappeared from the hall by the time she got up to leave—and Alicia was noticeably absent too.

'Come with me,' Matthew said tersely, leading her over to the lift.

Jessica hung back. 'I—Where are you taking me?'

His mouth twisted into a smile, his tawny eyes hard. 'Just somewhere away from this noise,' he mocked.

That 'somewhere' turned out to be his office on the top floor. He took her through the spacious adjoining sitting-room, switching on the lights to move to the drinks cabinet. 'Brandy, I think,' he murmured, pouring some into a glass before handing it to her. 'Where was your husband while all that was going on?' he snapped in a harsh voice.

'He—he stepped outside for some air,' she invented, sipping the brandy, and instantly beginning to choke as the fiery liquid hit the back of her throat.

Matthew came forward to pat her gently on the back. 'Good grief, girl,' he said impatiently, 'anyone would think you'd never drunk brandy before!'

'I haven't,' she choked, tears wetting her cheeks.

He raised his eyes heavenwards. 'How old are you? Ah yes, twenty-five,' he answered his own question. 'But you don't like to socialise.'

It was a statement that didn't really require an answer, so she didn't proffer one.

'Your husband likes to—socialise,' he continued, his mouth twisting contemptuously.

'Yes,' she acknowledged huskily.

'But you don't?' he persisted.

'No.'

'You didn't attend the dance last year with your husband, did you.'

Jessica evaded his eyes. 'No.'

'Why not?' he rasped. 'Office parties are notorious for starting—affairs.'

She looked up now, meeting his probing gaze unflinchingly. 'Are they?' she asked uninterestedly.

'Yes,' he hissed. 'Why weren't you here last year?'

Jessica looked down at her hands. 'My little girl was ill,' she mumbled, knowing she would have done her best to get out of it even if Penny hadn't been ill, as she had tried to this time, to no avail. 'I—stayed at home to take care of her.'

'But your husband didn't feel the same necessity?' he snapped.

She shrugged. 'It was only a cold, I didn't see why we should both miss the—fun.'

'Fun . . .?' Matthew repeated slowly, his gaze searching, disbelieving. 'Do you like to have—fun?' he asked softly.

'I—No—I——' She stood up. 'I think I would like to rejoin Andrew now,' she told Matthew coldly.

'No!' It was almost a shout, and Matthew was at her side within seconds. 'I'm sorry, I didn't mean to imply—I don't know what I mean any more!' he groaned in an aching voice.

Jessica only had time to raise startled eyes before she felt herself being pulled into his arms, his mouth slowly lowering towards hers. 'No!' She flinched away from him, but he just kept right on coming, his mouth taking possession of hers.

It was five years since she had been kissed by anyone except Penny, and that firm cruel-looking mouth felt strange on hers, his lips moving sensually against hers, remorselessly so.

Jessica didn't respond or resist, standing impassive in his arms until he at last released her. His face was white, his expression grim. 'So you do love your husband after all,' he said harshly, pushing her away from him.

'Yes,' she said emotionlessly, knowing that nothing could be further from the truth. She had stopped feeling anything but fear of Andrew years ago.

Matthew swallowed hard. 'I'll take you back to the dance.'

'Thank you.'

'Jessica——'

'Andrew will be looking for me.' She looked at him with unwavering eyes.

'Like hell he will!' he exploded. 'He—Oh, never mind!' he dismissed impatiently. 'I'll take you back downstairs, if that's what you want.' He hesitated, as if hoping she would say it wasn't.

'It is,' she said firmly.

They didn't talk at all going back down in the lift, both seemingly lost in their own thoughts—Jessica's tortuous.

Matthew Sinclair was the only other man to kiss her besides Andrew, and he had kissed totally unlike her husband. His lips had been gentle, searching, anxious to evoke a response within her, asking for that response.

And hadn't she felt the stirrings of that response, a gravitation to the warmth after so many years of coldness? Heavens, she was a married woman, had a child, and yet she had let a complete stranger hold her in his arms and kiss her!

But why had Matthew Sinclair kissed her? Did he think that because Andrew had affairs she was the same, that they were one of these so-called 'modern' couples who had sexual relationships outside marriage?

If he had he hadn't received the response he wanted. But the kiss had unsettled her, shown her that she wasn't as immune to physical warmth as she had always thought she was, as Andrew had convinced her she was.

Frigid, Andrew said she was. Well, she might be, but that one brief kiss of Matthew Sinclair's had shown her that frigid or not she liked to be held against another human being, to feel cared for, protected. After five years of Andrew's jibes and insults the other man's show of warmth, if not true affection, had caused an ache of longing she had thought buried deep within her, an ache for something she had never known—something she would never know!

She was married to Andrew, would stay married to Andrew, and despite the constant stream of women in his life she knew she would never turn to another man. Why face the name-calling and bitterness for a second time in her life? There was something missing from her body, something fundamental, that prevented her giving or receiving pleasure from any man.

'I'm sorry,' Matthew said abruptly at her side.

Jessica looked at him with pain-filled eyes, knowing that he apologised as much for what he had briefly thought about her as for the way he had kissed her. 'Yes.' Her voice was emotionless through years of practice.

'I have no excuse for what happened just now,' he continued stiffly.

They stepped out of the lift together, the dance sounding noisier than ever. 'It isn't important,' she dismissed, already looking for Andrew.

Painful fingers bit into her arm. 'It is to me,' Matthew ground out. 'I'm not in the habit of kissing married women.'

Jessica turned to look at him; his face was harsh, a pulse beating erratically at his jaw. No, he wouldn't be in the habit of kissing a woman who belonged to another man. The pride in his brow, the forbidding line of his mouth told her that he deeply regretted it had happened this time.

'I have no intention of telling my husband——'

'Your husband!' he cut in angrily, his tawny eyes blazing. 'I couldn't give a damn about your husband. It's *you* I'm apologising to, not him.'

'And I've accepted that apology,' she told him in a puzzled voice, not understanding why he was so angry.

His eyes darkened. 'Jessica—Oh, why the hell did you have to be married!' He swore before walking off, anyone who was in his path quickly getting out of the way.

Jessica turned away, knowing she had seen the last of Matthew Sinclair. She knew why she was married, why she was still married despite Andrew's affair—because of Penny, because of the one person who meant anything in her life. Every time Andrew's behaviour became too much for her she would take one look at her young daughter and know it was all worth it.

'Where the hell have you been?'

Andrew wasn't smiling charmingly this time, he was scowling heavily, and he wasn't alone either. Alicia was clinging to his arm—and looking as if she had a perfect right to be there! Her expression was blatantly insolent as she looked down at Jessica, at least six inches taller, and very sure of her own beauty.

'Jessica,' Andrew prompted impatiently, 'I asked you a question.'

She blushed her resentment of the other woman listening to the conversation, knowing that Alicia was aware of her discomfort. 'I wasn't the one who disappeared, Andrew, you were.' Her voice was more aggressive than ever before—but then she had never been humiliated in front of one of Andrew's mistresses before!

He flushed angrily. 'We—I only stepped outside for a moment. You were talking to Ed Taylor when I left the room.'

'I wasn't talking to him,' she mumbled. 'He was insulting me.'

'Ed was?' Andrew laughed his disbelief. 'The trouble with you, Jessica, is that you're too damned sensitive.'

And he was totally *in*sensitive! It didn't even occur to him to keep his wife and mistress apart, not even when he knew she was aware of his relationship with the other woman.

'Perhaps,' she agreed tightly. 'But I know when I'm being insulted,' and she looked almost challengingly at Alicia.

'I think she means me, darling,' Alicia drawled, her voice deep and husky, sexy, men probably thought.

Andrew frowned and gave Jessica a sharp look. 'Of

course she doesn't,' he dismissed, being used to a more subdued and obedient Jessica.

'Darling,' Alicia purred, 'why don't you go and get—Jessica and me a drink? I'm sure we would both like one.'

'I——'

'Okay,' Andrew cut through Jessica's dismayed protest. 'I won't be long.'

'Take your time,' Alicia murmured softly. 'I'm sure Jessica and I can find—something to talk about—a mutual interest, perhaps.'

Jessica knew that the only thing she had in common with this woman was Andrew, and he knew it too, giving a rather cruel smile in her direction before going to the bar.

'Shall we sit down?' Alicia suggested softly.

Jessica seated herself opposite the other woman, knowing they were the centre of attention. They knew, all these people knew, and her humiliation was complete as she saw Matthew Sinclair watching them some distance away, in conversation with another man, although his gaze was fixed on her.

She looked away before that fierce gaze gave way to pity. Matthew Sinclair's sympathy was the one thing she couldn't take right now. No wonder he had tried to kiss her upstairs in his office—he obviously knew of Andrew's affair with his secretary!

'Why don't you let him go?' The purring quality had gone from Alicia's voice, the hardness in her beautiful face now evident in her voice too.

Jessica blinked dazedly, frowning at the other woman. 'I beg your pardon?'

Alicia's mouth twisted. 'Andrew doesn't love you, so why don't you let him go?'

She swallowed hard, shaking her head. 'I don't know what you're talking about.' And she didn't. If Andrew had wanted to leave her she knew there was no way she could stop him.

Alicia was angry now. 'Andrew told me how you refuse to divorce him, that you use your daughter to hold him——'

'That isn't true!' Jessica gasped at the irony of it.

The other woman's expression was scathing. 'I've heard about women like you, I've even met a couple, but I can tell you now that you've met your match in me. Andrew and I want to get married, the only thing stopping us is you. I mean to have you out of his life, Jessica. I'm even willing to put up with the child to get him.'

'Child?' Jessica paled, her hands clenching. 'You mean Penny?'

'Yes—I mean Penny,' Alicia scorned.

'You aren't taking my daughter from me!' Her breath was coming in short disturbed gasps, her eyes huge in her pale face.

'Believe me,' the other woman drawled, 'I'd rather not. But Andrew is determined to keep her——'

'No!' Jessica's tone was sharp with distress. 'No one is going to take Penny away from me. No one!' Her voice rose hysterically at the thought of life without Penny.

'Here, calm down!' Alicia looked about them selfconsciously. 'Maybe I chose the wrong place to discuss this——'

'Anywhere would be the wrong place to discuss taking my child from me!' Two bright spots of colour heightened Jessica's cheeks. 'I won't let you——'

'Jessica, for pity's sake!' Andrew had returned unnoticed by either woman. 'People can hear you!' he muttered, sitting down.

'Really?' Her eyes glittered. 'And do you think they aren't hearing what they already know? I'd like to go home,' she told him coldly.

'I've just got you a drink——'

'I want to go,' she repeated firmly. 'Either you take me or I get a taxi.'

He frowned. 'Jess——'

'Then I'll take a taxi.' She stood up, moving with as much confidence as she could towards the exit, and took the lift down to the ground floor.

'Jessica!' Andrew caught up with her in the car park, swinging her round to face him. 'How dare you talk to me like that in front of Lisa?' He flushed with anger.

'How dare you use me?' she returned furiously.

'I—What do you mean?' he frowned.

'I've just been informed by your girl-friend that I'm the only thing stopping you marrying her.'

'And aren't you?' he snapped.

'You know I'm not!' she flushed. 'How many other women have you told the same thing so that you're free from any commitment to marry them?' she scorned.

'Hundreds,' his mouth twisted, 'and it worked every time. I just explain to them that I have this frigid little wife at home who'll deprive me of my child if I so much as mention divorce.'

'Well, tonight Alicia mentioned it for you,' Jessica snapped disgustedly. 'So maybe you just weren't convincing enough for her.'

His eyes glittered, his dark good looks contorted with rage. 'Maybe I didn't want to be. Lisa is my kind of woman—she likes to *act* like a woman,' he added cruelly. 'And she has brains too. Yes, maybe I just might marry her after all.'

'No . . .' she paled.

'Yes,' he said with enjoyment. 'The other women never meant a thing to me, but Lisa is different. I wouldn't at all mind being married to her. Not that you haven't had your uses over the years,' he added scathingly. 'You've been a good deterrent to marriage-minded women. That's the *only* reason I stayed married to you,' he laughed. 'You have little else to offer.'

His laugh was the final insult as far as Jessica was concerned. She had taken too much tonight already—Matthew Sinclair's strange behaviour, Ed Taylor's insults, pitying looks from almost everyone who looked at her, Alicia's 'friendly' little chat, and now this definite threat of divorce from Andrew, and so cruelly given.

Her hand seemed to rise almost in slow motion, hitting the side of Andrew's face with such force that for a moment he seemed to stagger.

But he soon regained his balance, his eyes glittering dangerously as he advanced towards her. Jessica didn't even flinch as he coldly, calculatedly, hit her back.

There had been too much violence from him in the past for it to matter to her; she did not even feel the pain any more. Andrew was one of those men who hit out when he was angry. For herself she had ceased to care, and as long as he didn't use that same violence on Penny she would continue to cease caring.

'I'm going back to the dance,' he growled. 'I could be home later, but then again I may just stay out all night. And I mean it about the divorce, Jessica. And you know what that means?' he sneered.

Pain contracted her chest. 'Penny . . .'

'Yes!' His smile was cruel in the extreme. 'You aren't a fit mother for her, we both know that. Lisa will be much better for her.' He turned and strode away, a tall, athletic-looking man with rakish good looks.

Jessica had ceased to be aware of those looks long ago; she knew only raging pain at this moment. Never! She would never allow Alicia to be Penny's mother.

The taxi-driver must have thought her very strange as

she sat silently in the back of the car—especially as he had to accompany her to the door so that she could pay him!

'Had a row with your hubby, have you?' he said cheerfully, handing her the change. 'Never mind, love, it happens to the best of us.'

'Yes,' she agreed jerkily. 'I—Thank you.'

''Night, love,' and he whistled tunelessly as he returned to his taxi.

Peg was frowning when Jessica joined her in the lounge. Penny was asleep on the sofa, her mischievous face angelic. 'Have you?' she asked softly so as not to wake the child. 'Argued with Andrew, I mean?'

She shrugged, having eyes only for Penny. 'I'll get her up to bed now,' she bent to lift her daughter into her arms, the small blonde head resting trustingly on her shoulder as she carried her up the stairs.

'I tried myself a couple of times,' Peg told her softly, following to fold back the bedclothes. 'She began to wake up each time I touched her.'

'I know,' Jessica nodded, smoothing her daughter's hair back on the pillow and tucking the bedclothes about her. 'She always does with anyone but me.' Her eyes filled with tears as she looked down at her daughter.

Peg frowned as she followed her out of the room. 'Is there anything I can do, Jessica?'

'No.' She blinked back the tears, leaving the night-light on in Penny's room as she closed the bedroom door.

'But you have argued with Andrew?' Peg persisted.

'Yes,' she sighed, 'you could say that.' She chewed on her bottom lip. 'He—he wants a divorce.'

'He *what*?'

'A divorce.' They were back in the lounge now, the tears at last spilling down on to her cheeks. 'Andrew wants a divorce,' she repeated brokenly, her face buried in her hands.

'*He* wants one?' Peg gasped disbelievingly, sitting down to put her arms about the sobbing Jessica. 'After the abuse you take from him . . .! Well, don't worry, love,' she said angrily. 'George and I will take care of you—and Penny, of course.'

Penny. Penny! Jessica sat up suddenly, knowing what she had to do. 'I'm going away, Peg. Tonight. I——'

'You can't go this time of night!' Her friend was scandalised. 'Come next door and stay with George and me for a few days, until Andrew comes to his senses.'

Next door! 'No, I have to get away,' Jessica insisted, standing up. 'I have to go somewhere Andrew can't find us.'

'Maybe he had just had too much to drink,' Peg encouraged. 'He'll probably have forgotten all about it by the time he comes home.'

'He isn't coming home—at least, not tonight,' Jessica said bitterly, and she knew that when he did he wouldn't have changed his mind. Andrew was determined this time.

'But where is he—Oh,' Peg blushed, realisation dawning. 'At least leave it until the morning, love. If he isn't coming back tonight there's no rush, is there?'

'No,' Jessica acknowledged slowly.

'Sleep on it, Jessica,' her friend suggested. 'You can't just go off into the night.'

No, she couldn't. She had until morning to make her plans properly, find somewhere to stay where Andrew couldn't find them. Besides, it would disturb Penny to wake her now, would frighten her. Things were going to be traumatic enough without Penny becoming upset.

'You're right,' she told Peg. 'I'll leave in the morning.'

'I'm sure you won't need to do that,' Peg patted her hand comfortingly. 'Once Andrew thinks this over, about how much you love him, I'm sure he'll change his mind about the divorce.'

How much she loved him . . .! She might have loved Andrew once, in fact she knew she had, but she certainly didn't love him now. Her love had been that of an adolescent who needed someone to care for her, and she soon realised the disillusionment of that.

'Maybe,' she agreed with Peg, knowing that it wasn't true. She had known it would end one day, had dreaded it, and she knew without question that this was it. Andrew might change his mind, given time, he had done it in the past often enough, but Alicia wouldn't. She was determined to get Andrew, and Jessica doubted the other woman was denied much that she wanted.

'I'm sure I'm right,' Peg encouraged.

'Yes, of course you are.' Jessica gave a bright smile, hating having to deceive her friend, but knowing that not even to Peg could she tell the truth. 'You go on home now, George will be getting worried.'

'Are you sure . . .?'

'Of course,' Jessica nodded.

'You'll be all right?'

'Yes,' she smiled.

'Well . . . All right, then. But don't hesitate to call if you need anything,' Peg offered.

'I won't,' Jessica assured her friend.

She spent the next hour packing her own and Penny's things. It was amazing how much had been accumulated, not so much by her, but by Penny, all of her daughter's toys suddenly seeming necessary.

She had called a quiet unobtrusive hotel in London and booked a room for Penny and herself, knowing she would have to get well away from this small eastern town. London seemed the only choice. It was big and impersonal, the place where thousands of people went missing each year. Andrew couldn't possibly find them there.

But he would look for them, she knew that. Whenever the divorce threats came up he always warned her that any move to take Penny away from him would be met by opposition. Not that he spent a great deal of time with their daughter, he just wasn't going to let Jessica have her.

She jumped nervously as the front doorbell rang a little after twelve, wondering who it could be. It couldn't be Andrew, he had his own key. Unless he had forgotten it . . .!

She frantically hid the suitcases and bag in her bedroom before running down the stairs to answer the door, still wearing her evening dress. If it was Andrew he was already impatient, the doorbell ringing for a third time before she managed to open the door, looking up breathlessly at the man who stood there.

'Mr Sinclair!' she gasped dazedly.

Matthew Sinclair looked at her with dark tawny eyes, his face white and haggard, his hair golden. 'I didn't get you out of bed . . .?' His voice was husky.

She looked pointedly down at the blue dress. 'No,' she confirmed softly. 'Is there anything I can do to help you, Mr Sinclair?'

He seemed at a loss for words, swallowing convulsively. 'I—I think we should both sit down,' he said at length. 'Could we perhaps——'

'Andrew?' she queried sharply, sensing something disastrous here, dismissing the idea that Matthew Sinclair had come here to carry on his flirtation. He would never be so nervous about that, and he was nervous, extremely so. 'Has something happened to Andrew?' her voice rose sharply.

'Jessica——' His eyes were full of compassion.

'Tell me!' She clutched on to his arm, searching his pale features for what he seemed unable to tell her. 'I—Is he—Is Andrew——'

'He's dead, Jessica,' Matthew told her in a pained voice. 'I don't know how else to tell you! There was an accident, and——'

She didn't hear any more; she fell slowly to the ground with a gentle thud.

CHAPTER THREE

When she woke up she was lying full length on the sofa, carried there by Matthew Sinclair, who now bent over her anxiously, his face pale.

Jessica looked at him with dull, lifeless eyes. 'Andrew—he—he's really dead?' she choked.

'Yes.'

'Oh no! She buried her face in her hands, crying as if she would never stop, then felt herself taken into strong arms, held gently against the firmness of Matthew Sinclair's chest. His shirt felt soft against her cheek, and she could feel her tears soaking through it on to his skin.

'Jessica?' he said some time later when her crying hadn't abated. 'Jessica!' he shook her slightly. 'You have to stop now.'

She shuddered. 'I—I don't think I can. I—I don't know what to do. My—my mind has gone—a blank.'

'You don't have to do anything,' Matthew murmured into her hair. 'I'll take care of you.'

She moved back slightly to look at him. 'You?' she blinked. 'But why should you——'

'Your husband was my employee. He was killed leaving a dance given on my premises. Besides,' he added gently, 'do you have anyone else?'

Jessica swallowed hard. 'No. I—Andrew is really dead?' she repeated disbelievingly.

'I'm afraid so.'

It was hard to believe all that life and vitality had been stubbed out in a matter of seconds. She might have been leaving Andrew, might not have been *in* love with him any more, but she had still loved him for being the father of her daughter. He certainly hadn't deserved to die.

She looked at Matthew Sinclair with haunted violet eyes, remembering the times she had wished she could be free of Andrew. But not like this, never like this! 'He—he didn't suffer?'

He seemed to hesitate, choosing his words carefully. 'Not as far as we know.'

Jessica frowned, sensing his reserve. 'What is it?' she asked sharply. 'What are you holding back from me? Is he alive after all? Is he seriously hurt, is that it? If so I——'

'No, it isn't that, Jessica.' The tawny eyes seemed pained. 'Your husband wasn't alone in the car when the accident happened.'

Alicia! She had forgotten all about the other woman in the last few minutes. She licked her lips nervously. 'He wasn't?' she delayed.

Matthew shook his head. 'He had my secretary with him—Lisa Barry.'

Lisa! This man also called Alicia by that pet name. An image of him dancing with the other woman instantly sprang to mind. Yes, he and Alicia had certainly been closer than employer and employee, in the past, if not now.

Her face remained impassive. 'Was she hurt?'

'Yes,' Matthew nodded. 'Quite badly.'

Jessica looked down at her hands. 'I'm sorry.'

'You're—sorry?' He sounded incredulous.

'Yes.' She looked up at him unflinchingly. 'You see, Andrew told me he had offered Miss Barry a lift home, but I had a headache and left early. If I hadn't——'

'You might have been with them!' he said fiercely. 'Which wouldn't have helped anyone.'

'No,' Jessica agreed quietly. Somehow she couldn't

face Matthew Sinclair knowing of her humiliation tonight, of her husband's wish for a divorce. Andrew was dead, nothing was going to change that. 'I—Thank you for coming here—for telling me. I—I'd like to be alone now.'

'Of course,' Matthew said stiffly. 'Is there anyone I could get for you? Someone who could be with you?'

'No,' she stood up with jerky movements, 'I don't have anyone. And Andrew's mother died three years ago.'

Matthew frowned, his eyes dark. 'So you're alone . . .'

'No,' she denied sharply. 'I have Penny.'

'Your daughter?'

'Yes.'

He sighed. 'You're going to need help over the next few days, weeks, and——'

'I can manage!' she told him firmly.

'Jessica——'

'Please, Mr Sinclair, I said I can manage!' Her eyes flashed.

He chewed down on his bottom lip. 'I'll call back tomorrow,' he told her finally.

'I'd rather you didn't,' she said jerkily.

'You can't cope with this alone——'

'I can cope!' Her voice rose hysterically. 'I always have and I always will.'

'Jessica, please!' Matthew held her hands in his. 'Let me do this. Let me——'

'Mummy? Mummy, where's Daddy?' Penny stood in the doorway rubbing the sleep from her eyes, her dilapidated teddy bear dragged along beside her.

'Penny!' she gasped, a feeling of utter helplessness washing over her as she looked at her fatherless daughter.

Strangely it was Matthew Sinclair who gathered the

sleepy little girl up into his arms. 'That's a pretty nightgown you're wearing, Penny,' he smiled at her gently, a big man who could be curiously soft and understanding with a child. 'And is this your boy-friend?' He looked at the tattered teddy bear.

This brought a smile to Penny's face. 'Don't be silly, this is Teddy,' she giggled.

'Did Teddy wake you up?'

She shook her head seriously. 'No, you did. I thought you were my daddy.'

Matthew's expression was grim. 'No such luck, sweetheart. But don't you think you should be in bed? I'm sure Teddy is tired,' he added coaxingly.

She looked uncertainly at her mother, obviously unsure of this unknown man. 'Yes . . .'

'Shall we take him back up to bed?' Matthew encouraged softly.

Penny chewed thoughtfully on her top lip. 'Mummy?' she asked.

Jessica had been watching in amazement as Matthew Sinclair charmed her daughter. Because of her sporadic relationship with her own father, and the amount of time she spent in female company, Penny often had trouble relating to men. With Matthew Sinclair she seemed to have no difficulty. Maybe it was because he seemed to have no difficulty relating to her. Whatever the reason, Jessica was a little surprised by the amount of time it had taken her daughter to question the unusual occurrence of a man putting her to bed.

'What do you think, Penny?' she said softly. 'Does Teddy want to be taken back up to bed?'

'Well, he is tired . . .' Penny still seemed uncertain.

'Then we'll all take him back to bed,' Jessica encouraged, more grateful to Matthew Sinclair in that moment than she cared to think about. The question of 'Where's Daddy?' could be patiently explained to Penny in the morning; right now the shock of knowing she would never see Andrew again was enough of a strain for her.

Penny was asleep within two minutes of being tucked beneath the covers, the much-loved Teddy held firmly in her arms.

'She's had it since she was a baby.' Jessica began to chatter as she and Matthew Sinclair reached the lounge. 'Andrew and I—When she was younger we tried to replace it with a new one, but Penny wouldn't hear of it. I suppose——'

'It's all right, Jessica,' Matthew cut in soothingly, 'I don't need conversation. Your daughter is beautiful,' he said abruptly.

'I think so,' she agreed stiffly.

'She looks nothing like——' he broke off. 'She's very like you,' he substituted.

'And nothing like Andrew,' she finished his unfinished sentence. As the years passed and Penny bore no resemblance to Andrew she had felt relief rather than chagrin. Penny's happy, often shy personality seemed to bear no resemblance to Andrew either—she only hoped it stayed that way. She lived in dread of Penny showing her father's violent temperament.

'Yes,' Matthew made no effort to deny it. 'Jessica, can I get someone to come in and be with you, a friend, or perhaps a neighbour?'

'No, I want to be alone.'

'I don't think that's a good idea.'

'I don't particularly care what you think,' she said shrilly. 'At work you may be omnipotent, and so used to ruling other people's lives, but I don't have to take orders from you.' She was coming to the end of her endurance, Andrew's death and Penny's suddenly asking for him throwing her into turmoil. She had so much to think about, to work out, and she couldn't do it with this man's interference.

'Jessica——'

'Would you please leave, Mr Sinclair?' Her voice was brittle. 'I need time to think to arrange things. I—Will Miss Barry be all right?'

'She was going straight into the operating room when I left the hospital,' Matthew sighed. 'She has a back injury.'

'Oh no!'

'Yes,' he nodded. 'It's touch and go whether or not she'll walk again.'

Jessica hung her head. 'I'm sorry.'

'Why should you be sorry?' Matthew's voice hardened. 'You weren't driving the car.'

She wetted her lips nervously. 'Was Andrew—Was he capable of driving?'

Matthew looked grim. 'I would say no. But only time will tell.'

'You mean—there'll be a post-mortem?' She swallowed hard.

He nodded. 'I'm afraid it's standard in accidents of this kind.'

'Yes,' she acknowledged dully. 'Andrew would hate that. Oh, what a stupid thing to say!' She gave a shrill laugh. 'He isn't likely to know, is he? I—You'll have to excuse me,' she gasped suddenly. 'I think I'm going to be sick!' She rushed out of the room, barely reaching the bathroom in time.

A soothing flannel soon cooled her brow, reminding her that Matthew Sinclair was still here, that he had just witnessed the indignity of her being violently sick.

'All right now?' he prompted softly.

She swilled cold water over her face. 'I'm sorry. I—I just felt——'

'I understand.' He turned her gently and walked her out of the bathroom and into her bedroom, pulling back the bedclothes. 'In you get. I'm going to call the doctor.'

Jessica froze in the action of sinking beneath the sheets. 'No——'

'Yes,' Matthew pushed her the rest of the way down, arranging the bedclothes comfortably about her. 'He can give you something to help you sleep.'

'I can't sleep,' she struggled to sit up. 'I mustn't sleep.'

'Oh yes, you must.' He bent over her, pinning her to the bed. 'You have your daughter to think of. If I leave you now you'll just lie here awake all night. And that isn't going to help Penny, is it?' he reprimanded gently.

He was right, she knew he was right, but for a moment she had forgotten she no longer had to get away from here, now the threat of Andrew divorcing her no longer existed. The guilt she felt at her relief made her start crying again.

Matthew's mouth tightened grimly. 'I'll get the doctor now.' His tone was harsh.

Jessica had no idea what the doctor gave her, but she did sleep; over the next couple of days she seemed to do nothing else. Peg spent all her time at the house taking care of her and Penny, and Matthew Sinclair appeared in the dreamlike world too from time to time, always kind, always soothing.

He stood at her side during the funeral, his arm firmly about her waist as she would have swayed and fallen. The sympathies of the other mourners passed over her head; most of them were friends of Andrew's, people she didn't even know. Alicia Barry was noticeably absent; she was still seriously ill in hospital according to Matthew.

Jessica's apathy had become habitual, partly due to the tablets the doctor had prescribed for her, meaning that she felt no pain, but then neither did she feel any other emotion, reacting to instructions rather than instinct, her eyes dull and lifeless.

'I'm sorry,' she said calmly when Matthew informed her of the other woman's still critical condition.

'Yes,' he sighed. The other mourners had left now, only Peg and Matthew remaining. Peg was in the kitchen feeding Penny, who had spent the morning with George. 'But at least she'll walk again.'

'And at least she's alive,' Jessica said dully.

He gave her a sharp look. 'I'm sorry, that was thoughtless of me.'

'No,' she shook her head.

Matthew's frown deepened. 'How much longer does the doctor intend keeping you on these pills?' he rasped.

'I have no idea.'

'Did you ask—No, I don't suppose you did. I'll talk to him myself.' He was pacing the room impatiently. 'What do you intend doing now, Jessica? Will you stay here or will you—will you move away?'

'I have nothing to move away to,' she answered softly.

'No,' he sighed. 'Jessica, I want to take care of you.' His expression was anxious. 'Of both you and Penny.'

She gave him a startled look, coming out of her apathy. 'What do you mean?'

His movements were nervy. 'You're incapable of taking care of yourself and Penny at the moment——'

'Peg——'

'Has a family of her own to take care of,' he interrupted firmly. 'It's been over a week now, and she hasn't left you for a moment.'

He was right. Peg had been very good to them, had taken Penny to school every day with her son David, and then come back to take care of Jessica. The post-mortem had delayed the funeral by several days, the results revealing that Andrew had been over the alcoholic limit for driving, and the accident had been completely his own fault.

But Matthew was right about Peg's own family being neglected, and with a son of twelve and a working husband she should turn her attention back to them.

'I'll stop taking the tablets,' Jessica said determinedly. 'Then maybe I can think straight enough to take care of Penny myself.'

'That isn't the answer and you know it,' Matthew scowled.

'Then what is?' she snapped.

'I told you, let me help you——'

'You've done enough already—and I have no idea why.'

'Don't you?' His eyes were a deep tawny colour.

'No,' she replied sharply. She didn't want to think about Matthew's motives right now, *daren't* think about them. 'Penny will be back from the kitchen in a moment,' she told him woodenly.

'And you would like me to leave?'

'Your being here confuses her.'

'Why?'

'I have no idea,' she shrugged. 'Maybe it's the fact that her own father disappeared so abruptly on the night you came into our lives.'

In fact Penny had run screaming from the room the first time she had met Matthew again after the night her father had died, an event that had been explained to her as tactfully as you could to a five-year-old who simply didn't understand. Matthew Sinclair seemed to represent the death of her father, and whenever he called, which was often, Penny quietly disappeared from the room.

'Then I'd better go, as you say,' Matthew said tautly. 'I wish—I wish—Never mind,' he sighed. 'I'll call you tomorrow.'

'I—We won't be here.'

'Oh?' He frowned his puzzlement.

'I'm taking Penny away for a few days.' Jessica's fingernails absently traced a pattern in the velvety cushion she cuddled to her.

'Are you well enough?'

'Of course. We're going by train, so it won't be any strain.'

'I could drive you.'

She shook her head. 'Penny wouldn't like that. Besides, it isn't far, just to the coast for a couple of days. Penny likes to play on the beach. This time alone with me will help her to adjust.'

'And will it help you adjust?' Matthew's tone was bitter.

'I don't understand,' she said in bewilderment.

'I'm sorry,' he said abruptly. 'But I can't help feeling—I'd better go,' he sighed. 'Please accept my condolences. Maybe I can call on you when you get back?'

Jessica avoided the intensity of his gaze, standing up to straighten the skirt of the demure black dress she wore, her hair like sunlight against its starkness and lack of style. 'I don't think that would be a good idea.'

'Why not?'

Her head went back. 'If you must know, people are beginning to talk! Even today—oh, they thought I didn't hear them, but I did. This is a small community, Mr Sinclair, and people talk. And right now we're the subject of that talk.'

His eyes blazed with anger. 'Your husband has only been dead a week!'

'That's why they're talking.'

'It's ridiculous!'

'Most gossip is,' she said dully. 'But it can still cause pain. If Penny should hear it . . . You know how cruel other children can be. She's already come home from school once this week in tears because some of the other children taunted her about her father being dead.'

Matthew groaned disgustedly.

'Yes,' she sighed. 'So I think it would be better if you didn't help me again. Penny and I will manage.'

'Will you?'

She straightened her shoulders determinedly. 'Yes.'

'All right,' he accepted huskily. 'But if you should need me . . .'

'I won't hesitate,' she nodded, relieved that he wasn't going to push the argument more. She simply didn't feel strong enough to fight him if he insisted, her small burst of energy deserting her as she abruptly sat down. 'Thank you,' she added tiredly.

'Don't thank me, Jessica,' he ground out harshly. 'I would have done the same for anyone,' he added cruelly, slamming out of the house a few seconds later.

Jessica was slumped back in the chair when Peg popped her head around the door a few minutes later. 'Has Mr Sinclair gone?'

'Yes,' she sighed wearily.

Peg came into the room. 'Penny's gone next door to be with David.' She too relaxed in an armchair. 'Was that Mr Sinclair I heard leave just now?' she asked curiously.

'Yes.'

'He sounded—angry.'

'I think he was—a little.' Her eyes appeared even bluer in her pale face.

'Did you argue?'

Jessica knew Peg had been a good friend to her, both now and in the past—and yet even to her she was reluctant to talk about Matthew Sinclair. He was an enigma of a man, a man whose personality and motives she just daren't probe. Before Andrew's death, at the company dance, he had made no secret of his attraction to her, hadn't denied that attraction even after he knew she was Andrew's wife. His behaviour the last week had been exemplorary, but the attraction could still be there, and she had no intention of becoming dependent on him, in any way. For the first time in seven years she was able to live without fear, to feel completely free, and she wasn't going to allow her gratitude to Matthew Sinclair to change that.

'Not exactly,' she evaded. 'He wanted to drive us tomorrow, I feel he's done enough already.'

'It was kind of him to offer.'

'I know that, Peg,' she sighed. 'But surely you've heard the talk? Goodness, if I have,' she derided bitterly, 'then surely everyone else must have done.'

'Mr Sinclair was Andrew's employer,' Peg defended. 'It's only natural that he would want to help you.'

'Is it?'

Her friend flushed. 'Well, I can't deny that when he took over the funeral arrangements——'

Jessica stiffened. 'He did that?'

'I thought you knew.'

Peg shook her head. 'I thought that you and George . . . I should have known,' she sighed. 'I shall have to talk to him about it before I leave tomorrow.'

'He was only trying to be helpful, Jessica.'

'I know,' she acknowledged dully. 'But if any of this gossip should reach Penny . . . She's been through enough already.'

Peg nodded. 'I still can't get the Teddy bear away from her.'

Except when she was actually at school Penny's Teddy never left her; the ragged stuffed animal had seemed to become her only security in the last week.

'She'll be all right once we get away from here for a few days,' said Jessica with more confidence than she felt. 'Actually, Peg, I—I thought I might move out of the house altogether.' In fact, the idea had been growing by the minute since Matthew Sinclair had mentioned it.

'Moving?' her friend echoed in a shocked voice.

'It has too many memories, Peg,' she sighed. 'For me as well as Penny.'

'Yes,' Peg nodded understandingly, 'I can see that.'

Jessica flushed at the pity in her friend's eyes. The walls in these semi-detached houses weren't exactly soundproof, and the sound of Andrew's constant tempers must have been clearly discernible to her neighbour.

'Besides,' she added briskly, 'it's only rented. And a two-bedroomed flat would be much more practical for Penny and me. Now I'd better go over and see Matthew Sinclair,' she said determinedly.

'Now?' Peg's eyes widened.

'No time like the present. Besides, I could do with the walk to clear the cobwebs.' Jessica stood up. 'If you could just take care of Penny for another hour?'

'She'll be fine with David,' Peg instantly assured her.

She breathed her relief. 'Penny is really frightened of the poor man.'

'Jessica . . .?'

'Yes?' She looked up with puzzled eyes at her friend's almost reluctant tone.

'Nothing,' Peg dismissed. 'It isn't important. Off you go—I'll tidy up here.'

Jessica looked with dismay at the debris littered about the room. 'It looks more like there's been a party than a funeral,' she grimaced.

'I'll take care of it.' Peg pushed her towards the door. 'Go and get some colour in your cheeks!'

Matthew Sinclair had a flat in town near his factory, and it took Jessica a good half an hour to walk there. The nearer she got the more sure she was that she would have been more sensible to have telephoned. After all, visiting his flat wasn't likely to stop the gossip!

Nevertheless, she made herself go on. Matthew had made all those arrangements without her consent, and she had to know how much money she owed him, and she intended finding that out face to face. Maybe now wasn't the best time to talk about money, but this was her last link with the man, after today she didn't want to see him again.

The man who opened the door to her bore little resemblance to the man who had left her an hour earlier. The dark suit had been replaced with fitted cream trousers and a dark green shirt, the blond hair ruffled into disorder, and he held a glass of whisky in his hand.

His eyes widened as he saw her standing outside the door. 'Jessica . . .' he breathed her name raggedly.

'I have to talk to you.' Her own voice was calm and controlled.

'Come in.' He opened the door wider for her to enter, his avid gaze never leaving her face.

His home was exactly how she would have expected a bachelor flat to look, very stark, leaving him the minimum of work to do to keep it looking neat and tidy. But it didn't look neat and tidy now, with clothes, both dirty and laundered, strewn all over the place.

'Sorry.' He hastily cleared a chair for her to sit down. 'I decided to go up to London for a few days.'

Jessica knew he had another home in London which he used when he visited his offices there, although the majority of his time was spent here. 'Then I won't keep you,' she said stiltedly. 'I just came to ask you for the bills.'

'Bills?' he frowned, obviously completely taken aback. 'What bills?'

'For Andrew's funeral,' she continued determinedly, ignoring the chair he had cleared for her, not intending to stop any longer than she had to. 'Peg has just told me you made all the arrangements, so I——'

'Thought you would come over here and insult me some more,' he finished harshly.

'No,' she gasped. 'It wasn't like that.'

'Then how was it?' he blazed down at her. 'Jessica, you certainly know how to throw a person's help back in his face! Well, don't worry about the bills, I'll make sure they're all sent to you.' He turned away from her. 'Now would you please leave?'

'I——'

'After all, think what the gossips would say,' he added bitterly. 'Your husband was only buried today, and already you're in another man's flat.'

Her legs suddenly felt shaky. 'I'm sorry I bothered you. And I do thank you for your help, I'm not completely ungrateful. I just——'

'Don't want me to do it any more,' he rasped.

She shook her head. 'I'm sorry.'

Matthew turned to look at her with tortured eyes. 'You know why I do it, don't you, Jessica?'

She looked away from the sudden blaze in those strange tawny eyes. She had seen that look too many times in the past from Andrew—the desire to possess, to subjugate. And never again would any man do that to her!

'No——'

'You do, damn you!' He swung her round roughly, his veneer of urbane charm fast disappearing as the blaze in his eyes grew.

Jessica cringed away from him. 'I shouldn't have come here!' she gasped.

'No, you shouldn't,' he agreed savagely. 'You know how I feel about you, Jessica. You know how I——'

'No!' She found the strength to wrench away from him. 'Don't touch me!' she shouted at him. 'Don't ever touch me again,' she warned him through gritted teeth.

Something like pain flickered across his face. 'Don't you know I can't help myself?' he groaned. 'That I've ached to be with you this last week, that I've longed to know you, to hold you——'

'Don't *touch* me!' she screamed at him again. 'What sort of man are you? My husband was *buried* today!'

'I know that.' Matthew closed his eyes as if to shut out the sight of her. 'And your daughter looks at me as if I'm some sort of murderer!' His eyes glittered like topaz as his heavy lids were raised. 'You think of me as a usurper——'

'That isn't true,' Jessica shook her head. 'I don't ever intend to replace Andrew in my life.'

'Never?' he groaned.

'Never!'

'I can't believe that,' Matthew said dazedly.

'It's true, Mr Sinclair——'

'Don't call me that,' he rasped. 'My name is Matthew. And I never think of you as anything but Jessica. My Jessica.'

'I'm not your anything!' she snapped angrily. 'And I don't think of you as Matthew, in fact I don't think of you at all!'

She knew she had pushed him too far by the sudden blaze of fury in his eyes; his nostrils flared, his mouth tightening in a thin angry line, suddenly pale beneath his tan.

'Maybe I should *give* you something to think about,' he ground out.

'No!' Jessica backed away.

Matthew didn't let her move far, his hands determined on her upper arms as he pulled her body into his, moulding her soft curves to the hardness of his, uncaring that he was bruising her.

His mouth was grim as it possessed hers, moving with an invading thoroughness over her unresponsive lips, becoming almost cruel as she remained passive in his arms.

She had known kisses like this before, punishing kisses that meant to inflict pain and humiliation. Andrew had kissed her like this when he wanted to show his contempt for her coldness, to show her that it was her frigidity that had caused their estrangement, not a lack of passion on his part.

She remained apart in Matthew Sinclair's arms. There was no possibility of her responding, her emotions switching off as soon as he had touched her, as she had learnt to do with Andrew.

He finally thrust her away from him, disgust for himself, and her, etched into his harsh features, his face pale beneath his tan. 'I'm sorry,' he said woodenly.

'It doesn't matter——'

'Doesn't matter!' he exploded. 'Of course it damn well matters!'

'Not to me.'

His dark gaze searched her calm features. 'No, I can see that,' he acknowledged bitterly. 'How can you still love the bastard——'

'You mean Andrew?' she interrupted sharply, wondering how everyone could still believe she loved Andrew after what he had done.

'Of course I mean Andrew,' Matthew rasped, beginning to pace the room. 'He was unfaithful to you.'

'Who has been talking to you?'

'No one,' he scorned. 'He worked for me long enough for me to know what sort of man he was. No woman at Sinclair's was safe from him. I had several complaints about his behaviour.'

Jessica turned away, her hands shaking. 'I don't want to hear any more.'

'Well, you're going to—'

'No—I'm—not!' she told him in a controlled voice. 'I knew all about Andrew's affairs, and—and it made no difference.'

'Jessica, I know now was the wrong time to kiss you, but I——'

'I'll never forgive you for what you've said and done here today!' She evaded his reaching hands.

'Jessica, for Pete's sake! I only told you those things because I'm desperate. Darling——'

'Don't!' she flinched away from him, her eyes once more dull and lifeless. 'I never want to see or hear from you again.'

'No!' He had gone grey now, pain in the tawny eyes. 'Jessica, you can't mean that! After a suitable period I want us to——'

'There is no us. And there never will be!' she told him vehemently. 'I could never love the sort of man you are.'

'Because I've shown you I want you for myself? Because I can't stop wanting you even though I know you don't want me?' he said in a pained voice.

'No,' she shook her head.

His eyes narrowed, a pulse jerking erratically at his jaw. 'Then why?'

'I have to go,' she said stiltedly. 'Penny will be wondering where I am.'

'And what about me?' Matthew demanded harshly. 'How am I supposed to survive without you?'

'The same way you always did,' Jessica dismissed coldly. 'I'm sure Lisa will be only too happy to have you visit her.'

His gaze sharpened, his expression wary. 'What's that supposed to mean?'

'Well, you had an affair with her once,' Jessica shrugged.

A ruddy hue coloured his cheeks. 'How did you know that?'

'You call her Lisa, don't you?'

'So?'

She looked at him with cool blue eyes. 'Andrew called her Lisa too.'

'You knew about them?' he said slowly, disbelievingly.

'Of course,' she nodded.

'And that didn't bother you either?'

She could never tell anyone about the blind panic that had filled her when Andrew told her he was divorcing her for the other woman. She especially couldn't tell Matthew Sinclair. Now that she knew that the attraction he had felt for her that first evening had grown stronger, that possessing her had become as much an obsession to him as it had to Andrew. She had already been through seven years of misery because of one man's obsession, she couldn't go through it a second time.

'No marriage is perfect, Mr Sinclair,' she told him abruptly.

'It would appear not,' he said grimly. 'All right, Jessica, you win. I won't intrude in your life any more.'

She could see that he meant to keep his word, and somehow that filled her with a sense of loss. She had never been completely on her own before.

CHAPTER FOUR

PENNY blossomed into a different child during their days at the east-coast resort, and Jessica had to admit to feeling more relaxed herself. It was years since she had allowed herself the luxury of dropping her guard completely, even with Penny, fearing that at any moment her daughter would be taken from her. Penny seemed to benefit from having a lighthearted mother, the air of foreboding that had surrounded her the last week disappearing during the days spent on the beach building sand-castles and eating candyfloss.

Except at night. The nights were different, and Penny's constant nightmares began to worry her. She would fall into a deep sleep of exhaustion, clutching her Teddy, and then would come the nightmares. Penny could never tell her afterwards what they had been about, but she could guess. The loss of her father was too traumatic to cope with.

On the eve of their journey back Penny had the worst nightmare of all, sobbing uncontrollably as she forced herself awake. She threw herself into Jessica's arms, her tears soon soaking the cotton of her nightgown.

'It's all right, Penny,' she soothed. 'It's all right.'

'Teddy was frightened!' Penny trembled in her arms.

Ever since Penny had been a baby her emotions had been related through Teddy. It had been endearing when Penny was younger, but now she couldn't help worrying if it were a psychological reaction to all the suppressed emotions Penny must have sensed around her. If it were she would have to show her daughter much more love than she had been able to in the past.

'Teddy has no need to be frightened,' she assured Penny softly. 'Mummy's here, Mummy will always be here.'

'Always?' Penny looked up at her with wide blue eyes.

'Always,' Jessica promised, smoothing back the softness of gold hair from the damp cherubic features.

'You won't go away—like Daddy did?'

'No, darling,' she answered huskily. It was the first time Penny had directly mentioned her father since she had been told of his death.

'Did Daddy go away—for always?'

'Yes, darling.' She knew that in something this serious she couldn't prevaricate.

'Did he go away with Aunt Lisa?' Penny asked tiredly, her eyes beginning to droop.

Jessica stiffened. 'No.'

'Oh.'

She moved back with a bright smile. 'Do you think you can sleep now?'

Penny was already snuggling down under the blankets. 'Teddy's awful sleepy.'

Jessica sat beside her until she fell into a dreamless sleep, knowing that she wouldn't waken again tonight.

Her own sleep was longer in coming. It hadn't occurred to her that Penny still remembered Alicia Barry, although her own single meeting with the other woman had left a lasting impression. At least Penny seemed pacified now that she knew Andrew hadn't left with the other woman.

She missed Andrew herself, although she was aware that half of that loss was the fear. She had lived in a state of tension for so long that she couldn't believe it was over, although she would never have wished it over at the price of Andrew's life. She cried for his loss when she was alone, missed his occasional moods of gentleness, his love for Penny.

But another man with fierce tawny eyes she kept firmly from her mind. She had no wish to even think of Matthew Sinclair, not after the way he had behaved at their last meeting.

Penny found the train journey back to Norfolk as much of an adventure as she had the journey down, and the week at the coast was a definite success. The bus ride from the station was another bonus as far as Penny was concerned, although Jessica wasn't so thrilled when she saw a couple of her neighbours sitting farther down the bus. Almost everyone on the estate had known of her shaky marriage, and it had made her distant from any of them but Peg and George.

Her greeting to the other women caught and held in her throat as she heard part of Janet and Shirley's conversation. '—only been dead a week,' Janet said with relish.

'And she's gone away with him, you said?' Shirley exclaimed.

'Well, they say he's gone to London, and Peg said Jessica had gone to the coast,' Janet said knowingly. 'But they left on the same day, and we all know how—solicitous he's been since Andrew died.'

'Is that what they call it now?' Shirley giggled.

Jessica listened in numbed dismay. Janet and Shirley believed, as did probably the whole neighbourhood, that she had been away with Matthew Sinclair for the past week! She looked down anxiously at Penny, but her young daughter was intent on the new book she had bought her for the journey. Thank goodness! This conversation was disturbing enough for her, without Penny hearing it too.

'Well, you can't exactly blame her,' Janet was saying now. 'Andrew was always out with other women.'

'I know.' Shirley, a busty blonde of Jessica's age, looked coy. 'He made a pass at me once. Still, I think she could have waited longer than a week.'

Jessica had heard enough, and got up to pull Penny down the stairs to the bottom of the bus. How could people say such things about another person? She and Andrew might not have had the ideal marriage, far from it, but she had more loyalty to him than to go away with another man a week after he had died. Maybe he wouldn't have shown her the same loyalty if the positions were reversed, but that was beside the point.

She was still pale when she got home, something Peg was quick to notice.

'Bitches!' she exclaimed when Jessica had told her what had happened. 'They're only jealous.'

The two of them were sitting drinking a much-needed cup of tea, Penny next door showing David the shells she had collected during her holiday.

'Jealous?' Jessica repeated sharply. 'What of?'

'You, of course. Matthew Sinclair is the catch of the county. Janet and Shirley would both give anything for him to show the interest in them that he's shown in you.'

'Peg, I haven't encouraged him——'

'I know that,' her friend said impatiently. 'I know *you*, Jessica. The poor man just can't seem to stay away from you.'

Jessica's expression sharpened. 'He hasn't been here while I've been away?'

'No, Janet and Shirley were right, he's still in London. But he did telephone.'

'Here?'

'No, me. He wanted to know if I'd heard from you, although I'm not sure he would have wanted me to tell you that,' Peg frowned.

'Because I told him to leave me alone.' Jessica could still vididly remember the last time she had seen him.

'He loves you——'

Her scathing laugh interrupted her friend. 'I hate to disillusion you, Peg, but Mr Sinclair has nothing so romantic in mind.'

'You mean——'

'Don't look so surprised,' Jessica chuckled. 'Men like Matthew Sinclair don't fall in love,' her voice hardened. 'They buy it.'

'Jessica!'

She shook her head. 'It's the truth, Peg. He thought I would be impressed by the fact that he was willing to take care of Penny and me—while his interest lasted. But I'm not impressed at all. Now can we just forget about him? I already have.' Although she wasn't quite so sure that was true. Matthew Sinclair hadn't kept his word that he wouldn't intrude into her life again, and if he tried it again in the future she would have no choice but to tell him exactly what she thought of him.

Penny went back to school the following week more readily than Jessica had ancitipated, and it seemed that children had short memories, because Penny had no more teasing about her father dying, and she settled back into school better than before they had gone away, starting to invite some of her friends back to tea, something she had never done before.

The next three months were some of the happiest Jessica had ever spent, and the small amount of money she received from the insurance company did a lot to compensate the allowances she received as Andrew's widow.

She began looking for a small flat and a job further in town, realising that she couldn't continue to delve into the money from the insurance or there would soon be none of it left. Besides, with Penny at school and no Andrew to cook and clean for, she had a lot of spare time on her hands, enough to fit in a part-time job anyway.

She had been for an interview only this morning that looked really promising, and she could hardly wait to tell Peg about how well she thought it had gone. But as soon as she saw her friend she knew there was something wrong.

'What is it?' she asked instantly, forgetting about the job. 'What's happened?'

Peg's face was pale, her movements nervy. 'Happened?' she echoed tautly.

Jessica searched her friend's face, seeing the lines of wariness there, the faintly haunted look about her eyes. 'I can see something is wrong, Peg. It isn't George or David?' Concern sharpened her voice.

'No, they're both fine.'

'Then what is it?' she frowned, her bubble of happiness fast receding. Something had upset Peg badly—and she had a feeling it was something that deeply affected her.

Peg chewed on her bottom lip, seeming to have trouble finding the right words. 'I—The rent man called this morning,' she said at last.

Jessica nodded. 'Did you give him the money I left with you?'

'Yes. But——' she broke off. 'Oh, Jessica, I don't know how to tell you!' Her eyes were beseeching.

'They aren't going to throw me out, are they?' Jessica joked lightly.

'If it were only that I wouldn't care, you could always move in with us.'

Peg had taken her joke seriously, and her trepidation grew. Something was very, very wrong here.

'I thought there had been some sort of mistake,' Peg continued agitatedly. 'I told Reg there must be a mistake——'

'Reg?' Jessica frowned.

'He's the man who usually collects the rent. Of course, you wouldn't know that, Andrew has always paid it straight to the landlord.'

She nodded. 'He's always paid the bills.'

'Has he?' Peg said bitterly.

Jessica's breath caught in her throat. 'What do you mean?' She felt a familiar sinking in her heart.

Peg looked at her with tear-filled eyes. 'Oh, Jessica, Andrew hasn't paid the rent for months!' She wrung her hands together, moving restlessly about the room. 'When I gave Reg your rent money this morning he asked me if I knew when you were going to pay up the arrears. I didn't know what he was talking about, so I asked him. He said Andrew had been warned several times about the money he owed, but that he ignored the warnings. I don't know what to think, Jessica.'

Jessica didn't want to think, she daren't. 'Did Mr—Reg say how much was owed?'

Peg looked uncomfortably. 'I—Quite a lot,' she choked.

Jessica didn't press Peg any more, seeing how embarrassed the other woman was. She couldn't believe this was happening, not again. Three years ago Andrew had stopped paying bills, and it wasn't until final demands started arriving through the post that she had found out about it. When she had questioned him Andrew had predictably exploded, telling her it was none of her business and that she was to stay out of his life, that he would pay the bills when *and* if he wanted to. For another two months she had worried herself sick about it. Then the latest affair had ended, and Andrew suddenly had the money to begin paying the bills again.

But this time there was no expensive mistress to

discard, and no Andrew to help repay the money they owed.

'I shouldn't worry about it,' Peg encouraged. 'It's probably a clerical error.'

Jessica knew that it wasn't. And she had a feeling it was only the beginning.

Four months later she knew the full extent of her debts. The three and a half months after Andrew's death had only been the lull before the storm. But three and a half months' grace seemed to be as much as any of the people who were owed money could go to, and it seemed to Jessica that each day brought new debts.

The part-time job in the local supermarket had paid off, and she now worked five mornings a week from ten until two, although she hadn't yet found a flat for herself and Penny.

And she was broke. Except for the money from her allowances and her job she had no money left at all. But at least she owed money to no one now. It was a nice claim to be able to make, but it didn't help her and Penny, especially with Christmas almost here. It wasn't easy telling a small eager child that Father Christmas didn't have much money this year. Penny had been through so much these last months that a good Christmas had seemed the least she could have given her.

Christmas Eve saw Jessica trying desperately to get a Christmas together, if only for Penny's sake. She had to admit she hadn't done a bad job; the tree was only small, the few presents she had for Penny were not expensive, but they were things she knew her daughter would like, and she had never believed in overwhelming children with too many useless gifts, not even at Christmas.

Her smile was bright as she waved goodbye to Peg

and George for the holiday. Peg's parents made it a tradition to have their three children and numerous grandchildren all together for Christmas. Peg had invited her and Penny to share it this year, but Penny was still a little nervy, and too many people at once could upset her.

'Can we do the tree now, Mummy?' Penny asked excitedly at her side.

Jessica dragged her gaze away from the fast disappearing car, smiling down at her daughter. 'Yes, we can do the tree now. You know where the decorations are?'

'Oh yes!' Penny's face was aglow as she rushed upstairs to get them.

For the next hour they put tinsel and baubles on the tiny tree, Penny eating more of the chocolate decorations than she tied on the branches.

'You'll be sick,' Jessica warned her as she went to answer the doorbell. Probably carol-singers wanting their money before they could even think about singing!

Penny gave her a cheeky grin, and it lightened her heart to see her daughter so happy. They would have a good Christmas even though they didn't have all the trimmings. They had each other, and really that was all that mattered.

She was still smiling as she opened the door, although the smile wavered and died as she saw Matthew Sinclair standing on the doorstep. She hadn't seen him for seven months, and she couldn't hide her surprise at seeing him now. He looked different somehow, older, with lines beside his tawny eyes, his face thinner than she remembered too.

'Hello, Jessica,' he greeted huskily, a fierce light seeming to burn in the depths of his eyes.

'Er—hello,' she returned lamely, leaning heavily on the door, conscious of her untidy denims and loose jumper next to the perfect tailoring of his pin-striped suit.

'I'm not intruding, am I?' he frowned.

'Er—no. Penny and I were just doing the tree. I—would you like to come in?' she invited nervously, aware that part of the embarrassment at seeing this man again was because of the assumptions Janet and Shirley had made about them.

He hesitated; he was no longer tanned, and his hair was like burnished gold. 'Are you sure you want me to?'

'Of course,' Jessica said briskly, stepping back to allow him entrance.

'Mummy, I——' Penny came to an abrupt halt as she saw who was standing in the doorway.

Jessica held her breath as she waited for Penny's reaction to their visitor. Penny had been so happy and relaxed lately, and she dreaded the scene she felt sure would follow Matthew Sinclair's visit.

'Uncle Matthew!' Penny's face lit up like the lights they had just put on the Christmas tree as she ran to him. 'You came too late to help with the tree,' she told him disappointedly.

Matthew was down on his haunches beside her. 'Sorry, little one,' he said gently. 'I was held up at work. But if your mother is agreeable, maybe you could come home with me and help me decorate my tree.' He looked up questioningly at Jessica.

She was too dazed to respond. Since when had Penny called this man 'Uncle Matthew'? And her daughter actually seemed to have expected him here tonight, had showed no surprise at seeing him at all. So much for her tension seconds ago!

'Come and see our decorations first.' Penny took hold of his hand, dragging him into the lounge.

'Is it all right?' Matthew held back, looking at Jessica.

She nodded. 'I'll make some tea.' And try and calm herself.

Penny seemed to know Matthew Sinclair very well indeed, and she had no idea how that had come about. Her daughter wasn't usually a secretive child, and she wondered at the need for it now.

She was setting the tray with the tea things when she sensed she was no longer alone in the kitchen. She turned sharply, finding Matthew Sinclair watching her with wary eyes. Her hands moved nervously down her thighs. 'I should have thought—Maybe you would prefer something stronger as it's Christmas? Would you like——'

'Tea will be fine,' he refused gravely. 'I think I owe you an explanation for Penny's greeting just now.'

Jessica thought so too. 'If you wouldn't mind,' she nodded coolly.

He came fully into the room, closing the door behind him. 'Penny's putting the finishing touches to the tree,' he explained indulgently. 'Over the last few months I've called to see Peg and George several times——'

She instantly stiffened. 'Why?'

'That's my business,' he told her arrogantly.

'Not if it involves me,' she snapped.

He looked at her coldly. 'Contrary to your belief, the whole world doesn't revolve around you.'

Jessica blushed at his rebuke, a rebuke she wholly deserved. 'I'm sorry,' she muttered, thankfully turning to pour the boiling water into the tea-pot. 'You were going to explain about Penny,' she invited stiffly.

'Mm. Well, a couple of times she happened to be there when I called on Peg.'

'And she just started calling you Uncle Matthew,' she scorned.

'No,' he sighed. 'It took a while for that to happen. At first she wouldn't even speak to me.'

'And now she thinks the world of you,' Jessica said

dully. And it was true. Penny's pleasure in seeing Matthew Sinclair had been undeniable.

He quirked one dark blond eyebrow. 'Do you mind?'

'Mind?' she frowned.

'That Penny has lost her fear of me.'

'Not at all,' she answered abruptly, picking up the tray. 'Would you mind?' She looked pointedly at the closed door.

'Jessica . . .'

She gave him a startled look at the intensity of his voice. 'Yes?'

'I wouldn't have come here if Penny hadn't invited me. I'm perfectly well aware of your aversion to me.' He opened the door for her, his eyes steely.

'Matthew——'

'Yes?' he pounced sharply, that light back in his eyes.

'Nothing.' She blushed, entering the lounge, aware of him following behind her.

Penny turned to them both excitedly. 'Doesn't it look lovely?' she exclaimed over the tree.

It did, in fact, look better now that it had the decorations and lights on it, although not even that could disguise the fact that it was a very small tree, and that it didn't have as many branches as it could have done.

'Lovely,' Matthew agreed deeply.

'Can I help Uncle Matthew do his tree now?' Penny looked at her mother appealingly.

'Well . . .'

'I really do need help, Jessica,' Matthew said softly.

She felt cornered, and he must know it. 'All right,' she nodded grudging agreement.

'Now?' Penny's face lit up. 'Now, Uncle Matthew?'

'That depends on your mother.'

Once again she felt trapped into her answer, although she couldn't really blame Matthew Sinclair. When

Penny was in this mood it was hard to deny her anything.

'Mummy?'

'All right,' she agreed indulgently. 'Go and get your coat.'

Penny rushed from the room, leaving an awkward silence behind her. Jessica chewed awkwardly on her bottom lip, still remembering the last time they had been together, although Matthew's distant behaviour gave no indication that he remembered it.

'You'll come with Penny?' he asked huskily.

The thought of going to his home filled her with apprehension, but she couldn't really allow Penny to go on her own. 'Yes.'

'Thank you,' he sighed.

She gave him a puzzled look. 'I don't understand.'

'Penny's—affection means a lot to me.'

She could see that, and Matthew Sinclair obviously meant a lot to Penny. Which made it all the more surprising that Penny hadn't mentioned inviting him here today.

Her daughter soon explained the omission. 'Didn't I give you a lovely surprise, Mummy?' she beamed. 'Now we aren't going to be alone for Christmas!'

'Penny——'

'I would be honoured if you would both spend Christmas Day with me,' Matthew told her softly.

She gave him a sharp look, as she sat in the front seat beside him in the gold-coloured Rolls-Royce. Andrew had always gone in for fast cars, but nothing like the luxury of this one. 'We couldn't possibly intrude——'

'Oh, why not, Mummy?' Penny pouted. 'Uncle Matthew is going to be on his own too.'

'I'm sure he has his own family——'

'Only his mother,' Penny dismissed. 'And she's gone away.'

Jessica had a feeling the ground was fast disappearing beneath her feet. Seven months of not seeing the man, and now this! It was too much.

Matthew sensed her unrest. 'Don't pressure your mother, Penny. I'm sure she has plans of her own.'

'No, she doesn't. We——'

'Penny!' he warned firmly.

'But——'

'Do you want to help with the tree?'

'Yes,' she mumbled.

'Then stop pushing,' he smiled to take the sting out of his words. 'Your mother will make up her own mind—in her own time,' he added warningly as Penny went to speak again.

That was easier said than done! Christmas was a time for children, for giving them happiness, and being with Matthew Sinclair seemed to be the best Christmas present she could give Penny.

Her agreement to spend the holiday with Matthew Sinclair had to be a foregone conclusion, although her reply was made warily. 'We'll help Uncle Matthew with his tree, and if you haven't worn him out by then maybe we'll accept his invitation to spend Christmas Day with him.'

Matthew turned to smile at her as Penny jumped up and down on the back seat. 'I think I should warn you,' he murmured, 'I don't tire easily.'

Jessica met his gaze unwaveringly. 'Then it looks as if you might have a couple of guests for the day tomorrow.'

His eyes became a light tawny gold as he smiled again. 'That's what I was hoping.'

Jessica noticed for the first time that they were driving away from the town, not towards it, and turned to look at him questioningly.

'I've moved into a house in the country,' he supplied abruptly.

Her brows rose in surprise. 'I see. I thought your main home was in London.'

'It is,' he nodded. 'Or rather it was. I've found I prefer to live here.'

She felt suddenly tense. 'So you live here all the time now?'

'When I'm not visiting my London office. I still have my apartment there.'

The house turned out to be huge, at least half a dozen bedrooms, a couple of reception rooms, and goodness knew how many bathrooms. The grounds looked extensive as they drove down the driveway, and there was a large orchard to the back of the house.

Matthew showed her round the house with obvious pride, and she could understand why. The house was beautifully furnished, comfortable rather than ultra-modern. Penny soon made herself at home, eager to start on the decorations.

'I'll make some coffee as we didn't get to drink our tea,' Jessica offered as Matthew indulgently let Penny tie all the shiny decorations on the five-foot tree.

He looked up at her, his hair looking gold in the overhead light as he lay on the floor handing the baubles to Penny, having changed from the suit into black corduroys and an open-necked blue shirt. 'That would be nice,' he smiled. 'Can you manage to find everything?'

'I'm sure I can,' she nodded, making her way into the modern kitchen. She had been amazed when Matthew told her that he didn't have a housekeeper, although he owned to having someone come in a couple of times a week to clean the house.

'Okay?'

She turned with a start to find him a few feet behind her, and at once felt selfconscious, especially as she was still in the denims and loose jumper. The clothes were serviceable rather than attractive.

'Fine,' she mumbled, turning back to the percolater.

Matthew moved across the kitchen to her side. 'Penny's enjoying herself,' he said softly.

Jessica could feel his body warmth as he leant back against a work unit a few inches away from her, could detect the subtle aroma of his aftershave. 'Yes,' she answered jerkily.

'She's a different child from the one I met almost eight months ago.'

She poured the coffee into the waiting pot. 'We'd both just gone through a traumatic experience, but children bounce back quickly, especially at Penny's age.'

'Does that mean that you still aren't over your husband's death?' he rasped.

Jessica gave him a sharp look, hastily looking away again at the tawny glitter of his eyes. 'I doubt I'll ever be over it,' she snapped, turning away to pick up the tray and walk into the lounge, leaving him no choice but to follow her.

She ignored him as he moved to sit down opposite her, his long legs stretched out in front of him, concentrating on supervising Penny as she drank her glass of milk.

'Thanks,' he tersely accepted his cup of coffee.

Jessica could feel his gaze on her throughout the evening, and yet she refused to look at him again, helping Penny put up the paperchains once the tree had been decked in its finery. Matthew seemed content to sit and watch them, making Jessica so selfconscious she almost slipped off the step-ladder.

He was instantly at her side, moving with lightning speed to steady her as she reached the ground. 'All right?' His voice was husky against her earlobe.

She moved out of his hold on her waist, still feeling the warm strength of his hands through the wool of her jumper. 'Yes,' she answered abruptly, delicate colour in her thin face. Her hair had grown several inches the last few months, falling silkily past her shoulders, giving her face a haunted look, and her eyes were as huge as pansies.

Matthew's breathing became ragged as he looked down at her. 'Maybe I'd better hold the ladder steady from now on,' he said gruffly.

His close proximity was the last thing she needed, and her concentration on the coloured paper chains was exclusive. She wouldn't allow herself to even acknowledge the way Matthew's body occasionally brushed against hers as she moved up and down the ladder.

'There!' she finally breathed her relief, looking at the finished result with pride. The room looked very festive, with balloons and paper chains festooning the walls and ceiling, the tree decorated and lit up in one corner, and what seemed like hundreds of Christmas cards strung across the huge brick fireplace. Matthew Sinclair certainly knew a lot of people. The presence of those cards reminded her that she hadn't sent him a Christmas greeting. Not that he would miss it among, this lot! 'Penny, don't you—Oh!' she grimaced her dismay as she saw Penny prostrate on the floor, fast asleep.

'She drifted off about ten minutes ago,' Matthew told her softly.

'Why didn't you say——'

'What would have been the point?' he shrugged.

It would have saved her ten minutes' embarrassment, that was the point! 'I'd better get her out to the car,' she said.

'Stay,' Matthew encouraged softly.

She blinked dazedly. 'Stay?'

'Stay here tonight, Jessica.' His expression was intent.

Warm colour darkened her cheeks, her eyes glittered furiously. 'I don't know what you think I am—I'm sure you've heard a lot of stories about widows, but I can assure you I——'

'Calm down, Jessica,' he rasped, white lines etched beside his nose and mouth. 'My suggestion that you stay here did not include the sharing of my bed. I have more than enough bedrooms to give you and Penny your own separate rooms.'

'I'm sorry. I just——' Jessica put a trembling hand up to her temple. 'There was talk before, and I—I couldn't stand it again. They thought—they said——'

Matthew moved her firmly to the sofa, giving her a gentle nudge to make her sit down before coming down next to her, his thigh very close to hers. 'Who are "they", Jessica?' he prompted gently as she continued to shake.

She looked down at her clasped hands. 'People. Neighbours. Oh, not Peg,' she hastily denied at his raised eyebrows. 'When I went away and you went to London, they assumed—thought——'

'That we were together,' he finished dryly.

Her eyes flashed deeply blue. 'Yes.'

'And how would "they" get to know you spent the night here?' he derided.

His derision was understandable, since the nearest neighbour was at least a mile away. But Jessica knew better than most how gossip circulated ,and she had no intention of spending the night here. 'They would find out somehow,' she said stiffly, standing up. 'Now I really should go.'

'You won't stay?'

'No,' she replied emphatically.

'I wouldn't touch you,' Matthew said harshly.

'You wouldn't get the chance,' she flashed.

'No,' he sighed, 'I don't suppose I would. And force isn't my way.'

Jessica had gone deathly white. 'Force . . .?'

He turned away. 'I just told you, it isn't my way. But I haven't given up, Jessica,' he warned strongly. 'I've given you breathing space, but I haven't given up.'

The walls seemed to be closing in on her, and for the first time in months she felt the return of the tense fear she had lived with during her marriage to Andrew. The last seven months without him had erased that fear, now it was returning worse than ever. At least Andrew had only been a mental threat since Penny was born, Matthew Sinclair promised to be a physical one.

'I have to go,' she said breathlessly.

'Yes, I think you do,' he agreed grimly. 'You still aren't ready for what I want from you.'

Her head went back. 'I don't think I ever will be.'

His eyes were narrowed as he slowly studied each finely etched feature, pale brows arched over deep blue eyes, small uptilted nose, the small but stubborn mouth, the body tensed as if ready for a fight. 'Oh, you will be,' he said determinedly. 'One day.'

'Never!' she told him vehemently.

'I don't intend arguing with you, Jessica,' he said calmly. 'Right now it wouldn't do any good. When the time comes there won't be any argument.'

'I——'

'Hush, Jessica,' he put gentle fingertips over her lips. 'No arguments, remember.'

'But I——'

'Be quiet, woman!' he growled, and bent his head abruptly, his mouth replacing his fingertips.

Jessica was too stunned to resist him, and that was all the encouragement Matthew needed. He deepened the kiss with a groan of satisfaction, gathering her into the warmth of his body, the hardness of his thighs telling her of his urgent need of her.

His hands ran feveredly over her back, tracing the curve of her spine, his mouth hungrily trying to evoke a response within her, to arouse her to the passion he wasn't trying to hide.

Finally he raised his head, resting his forehead on hers as his ragged breathing slowed to normality. 'No, you aren't ready for any sort of relationship yet,' he said gruffly. 'But I've waited thirty-six years for you already, I can wait a few months more.'

Jessica spun out of his arms. 'It won't change a thing—not a few months, not a few *years*!'

'Oh, I'm not waiting years, Jessica,' he gave a rueful smile. 'You seemed to need time, I've given it to you. Now I don't intend to remain in the background any longer. You're going to be seeing a lot more of me in future.'

'No!'

'Yes,' he insisted softly. 'And you won't be able to refuse me, because of Penny. You see, she likes me.'

'Is that why you——'

'No, it damn well isn't,' he rasped. 'I happen to like Penny. It would be hard not to, she's so much like you! And from now on I'm going to be visiting you a lot. I'm through staying in the background. I know it's what you want, but I can't stand it any more. Maybe I shouldn't warn you of my intention, but I somehow don't think you'll run.'

Jessica felt her horror increasing with every word he said. He hadn't forgotten her at all these last months, as she thought he had, hoped he had, but like Andrew his obsession had deepened, grown. Only she feared this obsession more than Andrew's. Andrew's had been the kind of obsession that would have—*had*—faded. Matthew Sinclair had the look of a very determined, single-minded man, with a will far stronger than Andrew's had ever been.

'I'd like to leave now,' she said firmly.

He nodded. 'I'll carry Penny out to the car. And, Jessica . . .'

'Yes?' She tensed.

'I won't always let you go this easily.'

She gave a choked cry and bent to pick Penny up herself. Penny instantly snuggled into her throat, completely knocked out from the excitement of the day.

Matthew opened the doors for her, picking up a pile of parcels from the hall table. 'For Penny,' he supplied gruffly.

'You shouldn't have——'

'But I wanted to.' He opened the car door for her, tucking a blanket around Penny once she lay across the back seat, straightening to open the passenger door for Jessica.

She got in without a word, staring woodenly in front of her on the drive back to her home.

Matthew turned to her once they were parked outside her house. 'I'm sorry if I've frightened you, darling,' he looked sympathetically at her pale cheeks. 'But with you I feel there has to be complete honesty.'

She swallowed hard. 'Tomorrow——'

'Is still on,' he said firmly. 'Penny is looking forward to it.'

He had done it again! He knew very well that she wouldn't disappoint Penny, that in her present emotional state it was easy to upset her daughter. The nightmares had almost completely stopped now, but Penny still had the occasional crying session where it seemed nothing would stop her. No, she wouldn't disappoint her daughter, not on Christmas Day.

'All right,' she agreed stiffly. 'But I won't see you again after that.'

'Oh, but you will,' he nodded. 'As much as I want you to. And I want to see you all the time. Do you have any idea what I've gone through the last seven months?'

'Gone through?' Jessica blinked.

'Yes,' he bit out. 'I told you I would stay away from you, and for seven months I succeeded. And it was hell, pure hell. I won't do it again. I want you, and I'm determined you're going to want me too.'

That was what she was most afraid of! 'You'll be disappointed,' she said dully.

'No, I won't,' he told her in a firm voice.

She looked at him reluctantly, recognising the desire and strength of will in his face. 'You don't understand,' she shook her head.

'No, you're the one that doesn't understand.' His hand moved from the back of her seat to her cheek, his thumb gently caressing. 'You don't know me well enough yet to know that when I set out to do something, I do it.'

'And you've set out to capture me?'

'From the moment we first met,' he nodded. 'Now let's get Penny inside. And don't lose any sleep over this, Jessica,' he swung easily out of the car. 'It will be for nothing.'

'Because you'll win in the end?'

'Undoubtedly.'

'And if the capture wasn't worth it?'

'It will be,' he said with certainty.

Jessica didn't argue with him; she already knew the answer. Any man who became involved with her would only end up disappointed. And Matthew Sinclair was going to find that out in time. The sooner the better!

He carried the still sleeping Penny into the house and up the stairs, laying her gently under the covers and looking down at her for several minutes, his face softened to tenderness.

Jessica followed him from the room. 'Matthew——'

'I'll pick you both up at ten o'clock in the morning,' he informed her softly, the bedroom door still open behind them.

'But——'

'Ten o'clock, Jessica. Be ready.' He didn't give her a chance to argue further, then left quietly, the gentle purr of the car engine disappearing into the distance a few seconds later.

Jessica couldn't beliveve this was happening to her for a second time, that once again she would have reason to fear a man. And without any encouragement on her part this time!

Penny stirred as she changed her into her nightgown. 'Are we at Uncle Matthew's?' she mumbled, her eyes still closed.

'No, we're at home,' Jessica answered softly. 'How else would Father Christmas know where to leave your presents?' she teased.

'Oh yes,' Penny answered drowsily. 'Has Father Christmas been yet?'

She smiled. 'Not yet, darling.'

'We are going back to Uncle Matthew's tomorrow?' the little girl roused herself enough to ask.

'Well . . .'

Penny's eyes flew open, completely awake now. 'We are, aren't we, Mummy? Mummy?'

'Yes, darling,' Jessica smoothed the silky blonde hair back from her daughter's face, 'we're going back tomorrow.'

Penny turned over into a contented sleep, a smile of anticipation on her lips. Jessica's own thoughts were much more disturbing, and it was the early hours of the morning before she fell asleep, a frown between her brows.

CHAPTER FIVE

Penny was up at the crack of dawn the next morning, jumping up and down excitedly on Jessica's bed as she unwrapped her presents. The doll and clothes sets from her mother were a great hit, the bedroom set and toy horse from Matthew even more so.

Jessica's eyes had widened as she saw the gifts, wondering how Matthew had known about the buying of the coveted doll. It was probable that Peg had told him; the two women had been shopping together when she bought Penny's Christmas presents. Matthew's thoughtfulness in taking the trouble to buy such a personalised gift touched her deeply, and Penny's adoration of him seemed to have deepened.

'This one's for you, Mummy.' Penny handed her the beautifully wrapped parcel.

It had come out of the pile Matthew had given her, so she felt sure Penny had made a mistake. 'I don't think so, darling,' she shook her head, knowing that Matthew's carefully bought gifts had added to Penny's day, and feeling grateful to him because of it. But he certainly wouldn't have bought her a present too—would he?

Her daughter frowned as she looked at the label. 'It has your name on it, Mummy. Look!' she held out the parcel.

Penny was right, the gift card read, 'To Jessica, love, Matthew'. The 'love' made her blush, because she knew the emotion he felt towards her was far from love.

'I know what it is,' Penny added conspiratorially.

Jessica's brows rose as she reluctantly took the gift. 'You do?'

'Mm.' Penny's eyes were bright with excitement.

'What is it?' she asked the expected question, her hand trembling as she held the parcel.

Penny shook her head. 'You'll have to open it and see. But I bet it's blue!' she added with a burst of excitement she couldn't contain.

Jessica swallowed hard, then slowly unwrapping the package, inwardly groaning her dismay as she revealed a beautifully soft sweater in an attractive shade of pale blue.

'And here's mine,' Penny picked up another parcel, proudly handing it to her.

Jessica put the sweater down as if it had burnt her. She couldn't accept such a gift from Matthew Sinclair—especially when she hadn't even sent him a Christmas card! But her anxiety increased when Penny's less professionally wrapped parcel produced a silk neck-scarf in the same blue as the sweater and a contrasting navy blue.

'Do you like it?' her daughter grinned. 'Uncle Matthew helped me choose it, that was how I knew your jumper was blue. Uncle Matthew paid for your scarf,' she added ruefully. 'But he said I could give it to you. You do like it, don't you, Mummy?' she repeated anxiously.

'Of course I do, darling,' she hugged her, her smile fading as she held Penny in her arms. 'I just didn't know Uncle Matthew had taken you shopping.'

'Oh, he didn't.' Penny went back to the toys she had unwrapped on the floor, having gone down early and found them under the tree. 'Aunty Peg and me—I,' she corrected with a giggle at her mother's reproving look, 'we met him in town last week and he helped me to choose it.'

'I see,' Jessica said slowly, not 'seeing' at all. It wasn't like Peg to keep something like that from her, but in the circumstances, the purchase of a present for her, perhaps her friend's silence was understandable. 'Well, it's beautiful, Penny,' she assured her. 'I thought so too,' her daughter said guilelessly.

Jessica took Penny downstairs to play with her toys while she went to wash and change. She stopped to look at the sweater and scarf again, touching them longingly. They were very beautiful, and Penny could have no idea of the cost of such items. But she could, and she knew she could never accept them from Matthew Sinclair. It smacked too much of buying into her favour.

But even though she knew the gifts would have to be returned she couldn't resist trying them on. The blue of the sweater deepened the colour of her eyes, her hair straight and golden against the light blue colour. The neck-scarf added style and elegance, and she looked very slender in the navy blue trousers she wore with them. It felt good to be so expensively dressed, and she sprayed on some of the perfume Peg had given her.

'Mummy—Ooh, you do look nice!' Penny stood in the doorway, having dressed earlier in one of her prettiest dresses.

Jessica blushed at being caught trying on the clothes. 'I——'

'Uncle Matthew is downstairs,' she was calmly informed.

She stiffened, looking at her wrist-watch. It was barely nine o'clock! How dared he arrive early——

'Very nice,' he drawled. 'You were right, Penny, blue is your mother's colour.'

Jessica looked at him with wide eyes, conscious of the rumpled bed behind her, her lacy nightgown lying across the chair. It was the latter she hurried to move, pushing it into the top drawer of her dressing-table, then turning to face Matthew once again, unconsciously noticing how handsome he looked in the brown trousers and cream Aran sweater, standing at Penny's side, his hand affectionately resting on her shoulder.

'Er—you're early,' she said jerkily.

He looked at her challengingly, having none of the distant manner of when he had called yesterday. And after their conversation at the end of the evening it would have been slightly ridiculous. 'Does it matter?' he shrugged.

'Er——'

'You can stay to breakfast,' Penny invited eagerly.

'Can I?' Matthew raised his brows at Jessica.

She swallowed hard. 'Yes—of course. I'll just change.'

'You look fine as you are,' he said in a firm voice.

'No, I——'

'Doesn't she, Penny?' he prompted the little girl.

'Beautiful,' Penny agreed generously.

'Yes,' Matthew stated clearly.

'Come and see what Father Christmas brought me, Uncle Matthew,' Penny tugged at his hand.

He nodded. 'I'll be down in a moment, Penny.'

The little girl skipped off, confident that Matthew would be with her soon. Jessica suddenly felt curiously alone with him—as indeed she was! A five, almost six-year-old was hardly a suitable chaperone.

'If you would like to join Penny . . .' she said pointedly.

'While you do what?' Matthew lounged in the doorway, his arms folded across his broad chest.

'I told you, I have to change.' Delicate colour tinged her cheeks.

'Why change?' His eyes were narrowed to tawny slits. 'You look good as you are.'

Jessica began to pull off the silk scarf. 'You know I can't accept this. It's real silk,' she put it down on the dressing-table, 'and the jumper is cashmere. I know the price of these things,' mainly because she couldn't afford them for herself! 'Penny has no idea, but you and I both know that I can't accept such expensive presents from——'

'A man like me?' he finished grimly.

'No!' she flashed. 'That wasn't what I meant!'

'Wasn't it?' He came inside the room, closing the door softly behind him. 'Take off the sweater and give me that back too, then,' he challenged.

'I——' she wetted her lips nervously. 'You know I can't.'

'Do I?'

'Yes,' she snapped.

'Why?'

'Matthew——'

'Don't put up barriers, Jessica,' he warned softly. 'You should know by now that it won't work with me. I'll just keep coming back, even if I get kicked in the teeth the first half a dozen times.'

'Oh, I haven't——'

'Haven't you?' he said harshly. 'Isn't giving me back a Christmas present, a gift given with seasonal cheer, kicking me in the teeth?'

'It's cashmere, Matthew——'

'I don't care if it's mink! The sweater was given with the same affection I show to Penny. You could at least have the grace to accept it as such.'

Jessica blushed at his intended criticism. 'It may have been given with the same affection, but it isn't as innocent!'

Matthew's expression became enigmatic. 'You think the gift has—ties attached to it?'

She chewed on her bottom lip, not fooled for a moment by the softness of his voice, his apparent calmness. Matthew was furiously angry, and she would be wise not to fan that anger. They were alone here in the bedroom, and with the distraction of her new toys Penny had probably forgotten all about them. By the glitter in Matthew's eyes she could tell he was as aware of that as she was.

She straightened her shoulders. 'If I thought that I wouldn't have let you in the house.'

'But you didn't—Penny did.'

'I was speaking metaphorically,' she said irritably. 'You've made your intentions clear——'

'Very much so,' he drawled.

'Yes. And I think I know you well enough to know you would never attempt to buy me.'

His light eyes mocked her, the dark blond brows high in derision. 'You do, hmm?'

'I think so,' Jessica nodded with more confidence than she felt.

He laughed softly. 'Think again, Jessica. If I thought my money, any or all of it, could bring you into my arms, then I'd use it. But *I* know *you* well enough to know that my wealth doesn't mean a thing to you.'

Once upon a time she would have agreed with him wholeheartedly, but these last months of struggling to pay off the debts Andrew had accumulated had shown her that there was a lot to be said for having money.

'What is it?' Matthew frowned as he puzzled over her shadowed expression.

She smiled brightly. 'Nothing. Penny wanted breakfast,' she added briskly. 'Would you like to join us?'

'If you wouldn't mind.'

'Not at all.' She avoided looking at him, finding that tawny gaze too penetrating for comfort.

'And the presents?'

'I—I'll keep them,' she decided. 'But I didn't buy you anything,' she said regretfully, knowing Matthew

Sinclair was the last person she had expected to see this Christmas.

The warmth of his smile lightened his eyes, easing their intensity. 'Jessica, with you I'm learning to find more pleasure in giving than receiving.'

'Mainly because I never give you anything,' she admitted ruefully.

'There is that,' he chuckled softly. 'But there's also the fact that it's more satisfying to give than to receive. Don't you know that?'

After the first few months of their marriage Andrew hadn't given her anything, not even his time if he could help it, and in the end her own giving, her taking care of him, had come to be a duty rather than an act of love.

'I suppose so,' she turned away. 'I'll be down in a moment.'

'And you won't change?' Matthew prompted softly.

'No. Thank you for Penny's presents, by the way. She won't thank you herself because she thinks Father Christmas brought them. But I thank you, it meant a lot to her.'

He nodded. 'I enjoyed it. I have a godson I buy presents for, but as he's now eighteen and into things like cars and stereo, it's some time since I looked at the toys on the market. It seems to be all electronics and computers.'

'Yes,' Jessica sighed. 'Which I don't approve of.'

'It's nice to know we agree about that.'

She frowned. 'It is?'

'Oh yes. Finding something for you was a little more difficult. I'd already bought the sweater when I met Penny; I guessed your size.' He gave her a considering look. 'I don't think I guessed too badly.'

He had guessed perfectly, and he knew it! 'You actually shopped for the sweater yourself?'

She could tell by the way he stiffened that he felt

insulted. 'Did you think I had my secretary do it?' he rasped.

'Lisa?' Her own voice was brittle.

'Quite,' he snapped, confirming that Lisa was once again his secretary. Jessica had heard, through Peg, that the other woman had recovered completely from the accident—obviously well enough to go back as secretary to this high-powered man. Had she also gone back to being his mistress? 'I don't happen to be one of those men who pass on such personal tasks to his secretary,' Matthew told her harshly.

'I'm sorry——'

'I should damn well hope so! Now let's have breakfast—Santa is in need of sustenance.' He took hold of her arm and led the way down to the kitchen.

Despite this lightheartedness Jessica knew she had really annoyed him this time, and considering his generosity to Penny and herself it was completely ungrateful of her.

Nevertheless, he appeared relaxed over breakfast, babying Penny by cutting her toast into 'soldiers' for her boiled egg, obviously enjoying the eggs and bacon she prepared for the adults.

'We'd better wash up, Penny,' he winked at the little girl. 'Mummy doesn't know it yet, but she has to cook the lunch.'

'Really?' Jessica pretended anger, joining in his teasing. 'I should have guessed I was to act as cook. It's Penny you really want to spend the day with!'

'Of course,' Matthew answered seriously as Penny gave an excited giggle.

'Then we'd better get going if I'm to cook the turkey for lunch,' Jessica suggested, tidying away.

'Oh, I've put the turkey in the oven,' he assured her.

'I just have to cook everything else,' she said dryly.

'Yes,' he grinned, looking very handsome, laughing

and teasing Penny on the drive to his home.

It was good to see Penny so animated, and Jessica could only feel gratitude for Matthew's interest in her daughter. She acknowledged to herself that not many men would take the trouble, even if they were intent on making love to the mother.

But the last thing she had expected to be doing on Christmas Day was preparing lunch in Matthew Sinclair's labour-saving kitchen! She had intended spending a quiet Christmas at home, and with Peg and George away it had looked like being that way. Then Matthew had calmly walked in and taken over, allowing her no time to regret the peace and quiet she had wanted. And if she were truthful with herself she didn't really regret the change of plans.

That the new arangements suited Penny she had no doubt, and she could hear Matthew playing with her in the lounge while she prepared the vegetables. She had been a little worried about Penny during this festive season, wondering how she was going to cope with the possible depression her daughter might feel at this first Christmas without her father. But Matthew wasn't giving her time to think of Andrew; he kept her fully occupied, her attention on the new toys she had.

Jessica wished her own thoughts could be as pleasurably occupied! Peeling the potatoes and preparing the other vegetables for the roast wasn't exactly a mind-consuming task, and her own thoughts did dwell on Andrew. Christmas had been the one time when he stayed with Penny and herself, both day and night. Except last year. Last year had been a disaster.

Penny had been up early as usual, bounding into her father's room to excitedly display her presents to him. Andrew had been suffering from a hangover and had angrily ordered her from the room, several objects landing against the door as Penny hastily ran to her mother.

Jessica had calmed the situation down, had explained to Penny that her father wasn't feeling well, and when Penny went down for her mid-morning nap, having woken much earlier than usual, there had been an almighty row between Andrew and herself. The result had been that Andrew slammed out of the house, not returning for lunch, and arrived home late in the afternoon, much the worse for drink. His barbs that day had been crueller than ever, his insults verging on crudeness once Penny had gone to bed.

'Mm, the smell of turkey cooking always gives me an appetite—Jessica?' Matthew questioned sharply. 'Are you crying?'

'I've been peeling onions,' she excused herself, wiping her cheeks.

Matthew gently swung her round. 'That isn't it. You looked very sad when I came in just now.' His eyes narrowed to tawny slits. 'What were you thinking about?'

'Nothing important,' she evaded.

'You're lying,' he said in an angry voice, a dark flush to his lean cheeks. 'You were thinking of Andrew!'

The expression in his glittering eyes caused a shiver of apprehension to run down her spine. 'Penny . . .?'

'Is playing quite happily,' he finished grimly. '*Were* you thinking of Andrew, Jessica?'

She moved her hands nervously down the striped apron she had brought with her. 'And why shouldn't I think of Andrew?' she challenged sharply. 'Christmas is a time for families, and Andrew was my husband.'

A white ring of anger edged Matthew's mouth. 'I'm well aware of who Andrew was,' he ground out. 'And *what* he was. So you miss him, do you?'

'I——'

'Even after what he did to you?' Matthew continued

fiercely, his hands thrust savagely into his trousers pockets, his hair slightly tousled from where he had been playing on the floor with Penny, giving him an almost vulnerable appearance.

Jessica stiffened, her breathing shallow. 'Did to me? What do you mean?'

He seemed about to speak and then stopped himself, swinging away from her. 'You admitted that you knew about him and Lisa,' he muttered.

'I did my crying about that months ago.'

'So you do miss him,' Matthew said dully.

'No! I—I'm over that too,' she added as she realised how callous she sounded. But she had admitted to herself months ago that her main emotion at being without Andrew was relief. She couldn't be hypocritical about it.

'Then why—Not more debts, Jessica?' he queried softly.

She paled, swallowing hard. 'You—you know about them?'

'Yes,' he sighed.

'How?'

'Peg——'

'I thought she was my friend!' she snapped, her eyes glowing with anger.

Matthew looked angry too. 'She is, that's why she told me. She thought I might have been able to help you. I'd told you I would be here if you needed me, Jessica, and you said you wouldn't hesitate. You did more than hesitate, damn you, you went through it all alone! I could have—well, I could have given you a damn good hiding—at the very least,' he added grimly.

'Peg had no right——'

'She had every right! And in the circumstances I should have guessed——'

'Circumstances?' she cut in sharply. 'What circumstances?'

Matthew shrugged, then quickly masked his expression, at once looking enigmatic. 'He was unfaithful to you.'

'It doesn't also follow that he wouldn't provide for Penny and me,' her voice had risen sharply.

'But he didn't.'

'No, he didn't,' she acknowledged breathlessly. There was something Matthew wasn't telling her, and a foreboding worse than anything she had ever known before washing over her. 'I want to know the truth, Matthew,' she told him in a strong voice. 'What circumstances? What else did Andrew do?'

'Do?' he dismissed casually. 'Nothing, as far as I know. How's lunch doing?'

'Matthew——'

'It smells good anyway. I never thought to ask whether or not you can cook,' he teased.

'Well, I can.' She still frowned.

'I can see that,' he smiled, his eyes warm. 'I'd better go and check on Penny.'

'Matthew——'

'Not now, Jessica,' he rasped. 'I don't intend to argue with you in front of Penny. We can talk later if you want to, but not now.' He bit out the words with slow anger, then turned to go back into the lounge, where Penny's giggles of enjoyment soon rang out.

Jessica managed to curb her burning curiosity until after lunch, when Penny had fallen asleep in one of the bedrooms upstairs, worn out from the day's events so far.

Matthew moved to pour himself a glass of whisky. 'Would you like anything?' he offered gruffly.

'Will I need it?' She turned in her chair to look at him.

'Not on my account.'

'But on Andrew's?'

He sighed. 'Maybe.'

'Then I'll have a sherry—thank you.' Her fingernails dug into the cushioned arm of the chair as she accepted the drink in her other hand, waiting for Matthew to tell her what she had to know. He seemed as reluctant to tell her as she was to hear it, and yet they both knew it had to be said. 'Please . . .' Jessica finally choked.

Matthew frowned. 'I'm not sure you can take any more.'

'I won't leave until I know the truth.'

'Then I'll never tell you,' he said bleakly.

'Matthew . . .!'

'All right,' he rasped. 'But remember, you asked for this. I'd rather not tell you.'

'If it had to do with Andrew then I had a right to know.'

'Even if it's going to make you unhappy?'

Andrew had rarely made her *happy*, so she wasn't at all surprised that what Matthew was about to tell her wouldn't induce the emotion either. 'Please, tell me,' she said quietly.

He sighed again, pacing the room. 'I have no wish to talk about this, Jessica. Especially today.'

Her mouth twisted. 'Christmas lost its charm for me years ago,' she taunted. 'If it weren't for Penny I probably wouldn't even bother with it.'

He scowled. 'I wasn't talking about Christmas, I was alluding to the fact that this is the first day you've ever spent with me. After I've told you about Andrew it could be the last. And I won't let it be!' he added vehemently. 'Your husband has come between us enough already, I won't let him take this away from me.'

'I've never belonged to you——'

'But you will—if I don't tell you about Andrew.'

Jessica shook her head. 'Not telling me won't make the slightest difference. I know you're keeping something from me now, and I have to know.'

'Do I have your promise that you won't leave after I've told you?' His eyes were narrowed.

'No,' she told him calmly.

He gave a rueful smile, a smile without any real humour. 'You're honest, anyway.'

'Always,' she nodded. She had had too much deceit from Andrew to ever want to hurt anyone the way he had hurt her, time and time again.

'And you want the same honesty from me?'

'About this, yes.'

'And you'll get it—you'll also get complete honesty from me about anything else,' he added grimly.

She blushed, knowing what sort of honesty he meant. 'Well?'

'Jessica——'

'Matthew, you've delayed long enough,' she said firmly. 'Now I want to know exactly what Andrew had been up to.'

'Fiddling his accounts,' Matthew mumbled.

She stiffened and sat forward in her chair. 'What did you say?' she choked.

He turned away, standing in front of the huge double doors that looked out over the neatly laid lawn and over the neighbouring fields, cows grazing peacefully in the distance. But Matthew's thoughts looked far from peaceful, a deep frown marred his brow.

Jessica stood up and moved to his side, gently touching his arm. 'What did you say?' she asked numbly.

He swung round, towering over her, his expression grim. 'Andrew had been systematically cheating my Company,' he told her harshly.

She paled, swaying, would have fallen if Matthew

hadn't grasped her arms and steadied her, leading her back to the armchair and sitting her down.

He stood beside her, his hands once again thrust into his trousers pockets, the shirt that had been revealed when he removed the Aran sweater pulled tautly across his chest. 'We had an audit of the books several months ago,' he said softly, not looking at her, his jaw rigid. 'There was a discrepancy found. We traced it back to Andrew.' He spoke dully, stating only the facts.

Jessica wet her lips, feeling sick. 'How—how much?' She looked up at him with haunted blue eyes, her skin appearing translucent, she was so pale.

He shrugged dismissively, as if the amount was of no importance to him. 'Several thousand pounds.'

'Several——! . . . ' she breathed raggedly, a hand to her suddenly aching temple.

Matthew seemed shaken out of his rigidity; he bent down on his haunches beside her, clasping her cold hands in his warmer ones. 'I didn't want to tell you——'

'How many thousand?' Jessica cut in as if he hadn't spoken, feeling nothing, not even aware that he still held her hands. It had never occurred to her that Andrew could have fiddled money out of Sinclair's.

'Jessica—All right,' Matthew sighed at the determination in her face. 'Over the two years he worked for me he took about five thousand pounds.'

'Five——!' She leant back in the chair, closing her eyes as if to block out this further nightmare. Only it wouldn't go away, couldn't go away.

There was no way she could pay back that sort of money. Five thousand pounds! What on earth had Andrew done with all that money? She didn't really need anyone to answer that, she knew the answer only too well. Andrew had always liked to live well, and when his mother died three years ago she had left him a small amount of money, a couple of thousand pounds. Andrew had spent that money during the first six months, on drinking and entertaining his other women, wanting to impress.

She had assumed that his change of job, working at Sinclair's, had given him the extra money he needed after that to keep up his extravagent life-style. When the debts had come to light after his death she had assumed it had only been them that had suffered to maintain his life-style, the expensively tailored clothes, the high-speed car. Now she knew she was also in debt to Matthew Sinclair.

'Jessica?' he prompted worriedly.

She gathered her scattered wits together, snatching her hands from his. 'Why didn't you tell me this before?' She moved jerkily to her feet, crossing the room to gaze across the same fields Matthew had found so fascinating minutes earlier—like him, not seeing a thing, her thoughts all inwards.

'What was the point——'

'I owe you money!' She turned on him angrily, her eyes glittering, with tears as well as anger.

'Not you,' he shook his head. 'Andrew. And he's dead.'

'I'm his wife.'

'His debt died with him.'

'Did it?' she said bitterly.

His eyes narrowed to tawny slits. 'What's that supposed to mean?'

'If all else fails . . .'

'Fails in what?' His voice was dangerously soft, enough of a warning.

Jessica remained undeterred. 'Yesterday you told me that you wanted me, that you were determined to get me. You also said that when the time came I wouldn't argue.'

Matthew was grey, his mouth a rigid line. 'You really think I—You believe I would——'

'I want to leave,' she said woodenly. 'Now. You'll get your money, Mr Sinclair—I'll make sure of it.'

'How?'

She flushed at his contemptuous tone. 'I'll find a way, don't worry.'

'Jessica, this isn't what I want——'

She wrenched away from his hands on her arms. 'I know what you want!' she snapped furiously. 'But you won't get it this way,' she told him vehemently.

'Damn you!' he snarled fiercely.

'And damn you!' She almost ran from the room, running up the stairs to get Penny from the bedroom. Her daughter was just waking up, looking sleepily adorable. 'Hello, darling,' Jessica greeted her softly. 'Ready to go home?'

'Home?' Penny blinked dazedly. 'I thought we were staying to tea.'

'Not today, darling.' She helped her daughter to her feet. 'Let's get your toys together and leave Uncle Matthew to his work.'

'Work on Christmas Day?' the little girl moaned.

'He's very busy——'

'Is he?' Matthew rasped, now standing in the open bedroom doorway.

Jessica turned to glare at him, holding tightly to Penny's hand. 'Yes!'

'Yes,' he sighed defeatedly. 'But he won't always be,' he added warningly.

She didn't waste time arguing with him, collecting up Penny's things within five minutes, looking pointedly at Matthew as she waited for him to drive her home. Penny sat in the front beside him on the drive, and Jessica was aware of those strange tawny-coloured eyes watching her often in the driving mirror. She ignored him, even though his gaze seemed to burn into her.

Penny's 'see you soon' to Matthew passed without response from Jessica. Her own goodbyes were made tersely; she was anxious to get away from the man who now threatened her very existence. Yesterday he had made her nervous, today he frightened her.

That fear kept her awake all night, going over and over in her mind how she was ever going to pay Matthew Sinclair back the money Andrew had taken from his company. Every piece of cash she could get together had been used to pay Andrew's other debts, and there was no way she could find a thousand pounds, let alone *five*.

It became more and more apparent that there was only one answer to the problem. Matthew Sinclair wanted her, it looked as if he was going to get her!

CHAPTER SIX

JESSICA had sworn that no man would ever have power over her again, that she was free of oppression now, and yet only seven and a half months after Andrew's death she had to admit to being a captive once again. And this time her captivity would be of a physical kind.

Matthew wanted a physical relationship with her, demanded one, and as with Andrew's mental cruelty she was going to have to give in to him.

She had made her decision and yet she didn't go and see Matthew until after Christmas, enjoying her time spent with Penny, knowing that once she had made her commitment to Matthew Sinclair her self-respect would be lost for ever.

Peg came back eagerly from the three days spent with her in-laws, generously offering to look after Penny for the evening while Jessica went out. Jessica hadn't told her friend she was going to see Matthew, and she hoped that even when she had made her bargain with him he wouldn't insist on making their relationship public. Although knowing Matthew she doubted he would settle for any hole-and-corner affair. It wasn't his way at all.

She hadn't told him of her visit, although the lights on inside the house told her that he was at home. She dismissed the taxi, taking several minutes to calm herself after the tail-lights of the car had disappeared into the distance.

Once she had stepped inside the huge oak door she would become Matthew's property, and the last few days of telling herself she had no other choice didn't lessen her fear. It was almost six years since she had slept with any man, and with Andrew as her husband she knew better than most of her own inadequacies. It was because of her lack of sexual response, her frigidity as Andrew had called it, that she doubted if Matthew would want her for long. She was counting on that.

Her knock on the door was tentative, and not surprisingly there was no response. A louder knock caused some movement inside, and she could hear Matthew coming towards the door. By the time he opened it she was completely tongue-tied, gazing up at him with wide distressed eyes.

'Jessica!' he frowned. 'What's the matter?' He seemed to pale. 'Not Penny . . .?'

She shook her head. 'I—I have to talk to you.' Her mouth felt completely dry, her words seeming to come out garbled.

Nevertheless, Matthew seemed to understand her, and he opened the door wide. 'Come in,' he invited huskily.

It was warm inside the house, and Jessica let him remove her coat, not surprised that he was wearing a shirt with the dark trousers. She was once again wearing the sweater he had bought her and so admired, this time wearing a slim black skirt with it, conscious of his tawny gaze on her as she preceded him into the lounge.

She moved over to the blazing fire, holding her numbed hands out to its warmth. This was going to be so much more difficult than she had imagined. How did you tell a man you had come to his home to become his mistress!

'Would you like a drink?' Matthew offered huskily.

It was so tempting to accept, to feel only numbed euphoria when he made love to her, but she had been a coward all her life so far, she wasn't going to be one now.

'No, thank you,' she refused. 'But you go ahead.'

'Will I need it?' he mockingly returned her question of Christmas Day.

'I—You might,' she nodded, wetting her dry lips.

He ignored the extensive array of drinks in the cabinet. 'Shall we sit down—or won't you be staying?' He quirked one brow.

'That—that depends on you.'

The intensity of his gaze deepened, seeming to see into her very soul. 'Jessica . . .?' he murmured softly.

She swallowed hard and looked down at the carpet, her hands clenched tightly in front of her. 'You told me I wouldn't argue,' she mumbled, 'and I'm not going to.' Her head went back proudly. 'You wanted me, Matthew, and Andrew having stolen that money from you means you—you've got me.'

His eyes darkened, his mouth tightening with a white-hot anger. 'What's that supposed to mean?' he rasped.

'I'm here to—to share your bed,' she moved her hands helplessly. 'To do whatever you want.'

'To be my mistress, you mean?' he said in a dangerously soft voice.

She nodded. 'If that's what you want. But I—I think I should tell you, you won't be getting a bargain. I've only ever slept with Andrew, and——'

'I don't want to know about the men you've slept with!' he exploded, tense with fury. 'Especially Andrew,' he scowled. 'You know damn well that the thought of any other man within a hundred miles of you tears me apart!'

Yes, she knew he wanted her with a fierceness that amounted to obsession. It was because of this she believed she might be able to cope with the trauma of being his mistress. He wanted her, cared nothing for the fact that she didn't return his desire, and no doubt his lovemaking would be as selfish as Andrew's had been. She had suffered two years of Andrew's invasion of her body, surely she could bear a few weeks of Matthew's selfish passion? She told herself she could, she just wanted to get it over with.

'I only wanted to explain that I'm not experienced,' she said stiffly. 'Shall we get on with it.'

His eyes narrowed. 'Now?'

She shrugged. 'Why not?'

Matthew moved to the fireplace, one hand resting on the high mantel as he gazed down at the flickering flames. 'Let me get this straight,' he finally said flatly. 'You're offering yourself to me because of five thousand pounds Andrew took from my Company?'

'Yes.'

'And you're without experience, you said?'

She blushed. 'Yes.'

His mouth twisted mockingly. 'Then isn't it expecting a bit much to think that I'll pay five thousand pounds for your body?'

Jessica flushed at his intended insult. He was trying to wound—and he was succeeding. 'Unlimited use,' she mumbled.

'What does that mean?'

'It means that I'll be your mistress for as long as you want me,' she told him dully.

'As long as I want you?' he echoed sharply.

'Yes.' She was confident it wouldn't be for long.

'And the—affair starts now?' he said softly.

Jessica swallowed hard, beginning to feel lightheaded. This was so much more humiliating than she had ever imagined. Why didn't he just make love to her and get it over with! 'Yes,' she nodded.

'Right now?'

'Oh, for goodness' sake!' her control snapped. 'Do you want me or don't you?'

'I—want you,' he nodded.

'Then let's not play games. You've got what you want, so let's get on with it.' She was shaking so badly she wasn't sure she was going to be able to move when the time came. 'Shall we go upstairs?'

'Why bother to go upstairs?' Matthew moved with his cat-like tread to switch off the two lamps that had been the room's only lighting. 'I think it would be much more romantic to make love to you here in the firelight.'

'Here?' She blinked dazedly, looking down at the fluffy goatskin rug in front of the fire, then her eyes widened as Matthew lowered his long length down at her feet, holding out his hand invitingly.

'Jessica?' he prompted softly.

Somehow this wasn't going as she had thought it would, clinically going to bed with him and then leaving bearing little resemblance to reality. Desire shone in the tawny eyes, desire and passion, and his mouth curved into a satisfied smile, looking very attractive in the fire's flickering light, his hair gleaming goldly.

'Come here,' he instructed gruffly.

He had a perfect right to order her around, in fact she would prefer it if he did. This way there would be no chance of her forgetting she was the slave, here through no choice of her own, and he was the master.

She sank slowly on to the rug beside him, at once breathless by his closeness, the male smell of him mixed up with tangy aftershave. She flinched as his hand moved to cup her cheek, turning her face so that she was looking at him completely by the time his mouth lowered on to hers. As always she didn't respond, couldn't respond, and she lay stiffly in his arms as he lowered her to the floor, leaning over her seductively.

'Kiss me back, Jessica,' he murmured against her mouth, his hand on her chin holding her immovable.

'I——'

'Kiss me. Touch me. Do all the things to me I've been dreaming you would do ever since I first saw you!' he groaned.

'I——'

'Do it, Jessica,' he said shakily, his mouth claiming hers while he guided her hands to his body, undoing the buttons to his shirt as she hesitated. 'Kiss me,' his mouth moved against her throat, biting erotically along the sensitive line of her jaw.

She reacted to orders, her mouth moving over the muscled firmness of his chest, feeling the roughness of the dark blond hair growing there, the hardness of his male nipples as her lips moved over them.

'Lower, Jessica,' he invited. 'Kiss me lower.' He rolled over on to his back, taking her with him, undoing the fastening of his trousers before telling her to remove them. 'Help me,' he encouraged as she stared at him in numbed silence.

He was shrugging his broad shoulders out of his shirt by the time she turned from putting his trousers to one side, and her eyes widened with shock as he lay naked before her.

But not for long, as he sat up to pull her sweater over her head, dispensing with her skirt as efficiently as he did her undergarments. Now he was kissing her in earnest, his body covering hers as his mouth lowered to her breasts, tasting the nipples as if they were nectar to him.

Jessica felt the response of her body to his surging thighs so close to her own, and yet part of her still stayed aloof, refusing to respond, unable to respond. The tears came unbidden, trickling quietly down her cheeks as Matthew continued his caresses, seemingly unaware of her distress.

'I've waited so long for this,' he groaned against her

earlobe, his hands holding her thighs against his, the hardness of his flesh almost hurting her, leaving her in no doubt that his control had gone completely, that there could be only one outcome to this encounter. 'Jessica?' he raised his head at her silence, frowning as he saw her tears. 'It isn't what you want, though, is it?' he said huskily.

She bit her bottom lip to hold back the sobs. 'I——'

'And it isn't really what I want either.' He grimly levered himself away from her, pulling on his clothes without haste.

'Matthew?' She sat up dazedly, hardly able to believe he had turned his emotions off so abruptly. 'You don't want me?' she frowned. 'But you said——'

'I do want you,' he gently helped her on with her clothes, smoothing her hair away from her face as he framed it with his hands, 'but not like this,' he knelt in front of her. 'Do you really want to go sneaking around, snatching a few hours together here and there, making everything sordid?'

Jessica didn't see how it could possibly be any more sordid than it already was! 'No . . .'

'Neither do I,' he told her grimly.

'But just now——'

'You had offered to give me what I've desired for the past eight months.' He stood up, taking her with him, putting her firmly into one of the armchairs before her legs threatened not to support her. 'Of course I lost my head.' His smile was gentle.

'But if you don't want that . . .'

'What do I want?' he finished derisively. 'Certainly not a part-time lover.' He stood very tall and dominating, a man who knew exactly what he wanted, and would let nothing stand in his way. 'Being a lover gives you freedom——'

'You too,' she pointed out heatedly. Why couldn't this

have turned out as emotional and cold-blooded as it had seemed! Instead of which Matthew was making her aware of just how cheaply she had acted just now. Cheap?—Five thousand pounds could hardly be called cheap!

'Freedom I don't want,' he told her firmly. 'And freedom I don't intend you to have. I don't want you as my mistress, my lover, or any other transient form of relationship.'

'You don't?' she frowned her puzzlement.

'No,' he said confidently. 'I'm looking for a wife, Jessica, someone to share my bed on a full-time basis. And I want you to be that wife.'

CHAPTER SEVEN

'Wife?' she gasped. 'You mean you want to—*marry* me?'

Matthew's mouth twisted. 'Do you know of any other way you can become my wife?'

'No!' She stood up as if to flee, her face taking on a haunted look.

Matthew's expression became fierce, a threatening glitter to his eyes. 'What do you mean, no?'

'I don't want to be married——'

'Did you hear me ask you?'

'No . . .'

'And I'm not going to,' he bit out. 'I want to marry you, you've admitted you're in debt to me——'

'Not enough to marry you!'

'No?'

'No!' her eyes blazed.

He shrugged. 'I'll make the arrangements——'

'I said I don't want to get married!'

His expression became thoughtful, his slow appraisal making her blush. 'You don't want to get married, period? Or you don't want to marry me, specifically?'

'Both!'

'Pity,' he drawled without sympathy. 'I told you, I'm not asking, I'm telling.'

Jessica searched his face, seeing only calm tawny eyes, the brows raised questioningly, his expression one of bland acceptance; all his anger was gone, confidence sat in every taut line of his body. 'I—I can't,' she choked. But she was aware her voice lacked conviction, and she knew Matthew was aware of it too; triumph shone in his eyes.

'There's no way that you won't,' he said with certainty. 'Believe me, Jessica, I'm not usually this domineering,' he added gently. 'But with you I have to be. Surely you can see it's the obvious answer, that you and Penny can't go on alone any longer,' he added coaxingly.

'I've only been widowed eight months,' she protested. 'I can't possibly marry anyone yet. How could I explain to Penny when she's older? I can't——'

'If it's your sense of propriety that's outraged I'll wait the year,' he stated flatly.

Jessica blinked. 'You will?'

'If that's what you want,' he nodded.

'I—Wouldn't that be hypocritical?'

'I think so, but that's up to you,' he shrugged.

'*I* would rather not get married at all.'

'You would rather settle for the affair?' His eyes were narrowed.

She paled, remembering how degraded she had felt while Matthew made love to her, her sense of utter helplessness. But would she have any more self-respect being his wife?

'How long would I—would we be married?'

'Permanently,' he said in an uncompromising tone.

'What if you—fell in love with someone else?'

His mouth twisted. 'I've reached the age of thirty-six without meeting the woman I love, I doubt I'll meet her at this late date.'

'But if you do?' she persisted.

'I'll let you know,' he mocked. 'Think of Penny's future, Jessica, the things I could give her—as her father.'

Jessica swallowed hard. As usual Matthew had found her weak spot. Penny's happiness came first with her, it had since the day she was born, and there had been too many things lately that Penny had had to do without, even a trip by the school stretching her purse-strings. As Penny grew older these monetary demands would get higher, and she didn't know if she was right to deny her daughter the pleasure of being able to join in.

But would she be able to stand being Matthew's wife? She had been Andrew's, and Matthew was so much stronger than him, so much more reliable.

'Yes,' she agreed flatly.

'Yes?' he asked warily.

'I'll marry you,' she told him huskily.

'When?'

'As soon as you make the arrangements.'

He swallowed hard, showing that he hadn't been as confident of her answer as he appeared to be. 'I'll give you your year, Jessica,' he said throatily.

Her eyes widened disbelievingly. Minutes ago he had seemed determined that they shouldn't wait at all. Why had he changed his mind?

'I have to answer to Penny too one day,' he explained ruefully. 'And any other children we might have,' he added softly, almost challengingly.

Colour flooded her cheeks. 'You want children?'

'Dozens,' he nodded.

She gave a nervous laugh. 'Isn't that rather ambitious?'

'I don't think so.' His eyes narrowed. 'Do you have any objection to giving me children?'

'I—None at all,' she shook her head. Pregnancy might give her a respite from sharing his bed.

His mouth twisted derisively. 'And I have no objection to giving them to you. In fact, I'm sure I'll enjoy it.'

Jessica's embarrassment deepened, and she quickly changed the subject. 'Will we live here?'

'Why not?' he shrugged. 'I bought the house for you.'

'For—for me?' she choked disbelievingly.

Matthew nodded. 'The apartment was fine for me while I was single, but as soon as I decided to marry you I knew I would have to look for somewhere bigger. Penny will benefit from the garden. She can even have a horse if she wants one.'

'She's frightened of them,' Jessica told him absently. He had been so sure of marrying her that he had even gone out and bought this house! She wasn't sure she liked such confidence.

'Only because she's never had anything to do with them,' he dismissed, having no idea how disturbed her thoughts were. 'I'll get her a little pony and teach her to ride. I'd also like to adopt her as my own one day,' he added tersely.

Jessica looked up at him with a start. 'Penny likes you, but—isn't adoption a little premature?'

'I don't see why.'

'Well—But——'

'She's going to be my daughter, Jessica,' he said implacably. 'And you're going to be my wife.'

'But——'

'I don't intend for there to be one fragment of Andrew Baxter still in your life once you're mine,' he told her fiercely. 'I intend to obliterate him from your life!'

Jessica wished that were possible, wished she could forget all the hurt and distrust she had known from Andrew, but over the next few months that proved to be as impossible as accepting Matthew's gentle concern and contrasting raging passion.

They met most evenings after the night she agreed to marry him, spent all of their weekends together, and Matthew never lost an opportunity of showing her his blistering desire to possess her. It angered him that she would never respond, and one night he really lost his temper with her.

'What the hell is the matter with you?' He thrust himself up from the sofa, where seconds before he had been intent on making love to her, turning on her savagely, very dark and virile with his shirt partly unbuttoned down his chest, his fair hair falling untidily across his furrowed brow. 'I'm going to marry you, Jessica,' he snapped. 'I'm not trying to rape you!'

She knew that, knew him well enough now to know he would never hurt or humiliate her in that way. Over the last few months she had come to know the man who was to be her husband, had a respect for him that bordered on genuine liking. It *would* be genuine liking if it weren't for the fact that she knew in a month's time this man would have complete authority over her and her life.

'What is it?' He came down on his haunches beside her, stilling her nervous straightening of her clothes, leaving the last few buttons of her blouse open, the smooth curve of her breasts visible to him. 'Do you hate my touch so much?' His light gaze searched the paleness of her face.

She didn't hate him at all, in fact a couple of times lately she had enjoyed his caresses. And that frightened her too. Once she had responded with abandon to Andrew's lovemaking, and only once—his taunts had made her recoil from ever doing so again.

'Jessica!' Matthew mistook her silence for assent, standing up with a savage movement. 'Do you want to call off the wedding?' He looked down at her.

She swallowed hard. 'Do you?'

'You know damned well I don't,' he rasped, deep lines grooved into his lean cheeks beside his mouth.

'Then we won't.' Was that relief she felt? Did she actually want to marry him? Surely not!

'I'll make you a good husband, Jessica,' he told her

intently. 'I'll care for you and Penny, neither of you will ever go short of anything.'

'I know that,' she answered almost warily, sure that there was more.

'But everything has a price,' he added grimly, confirming her suspicions. 'And knowing you hate it every time I touch you is going to kill me!'

'I don't hate it.' Her hands were clenched together. 'I just—I need time—to adjust——'

'To my lovemaking instead of Andrew's?' Matthew said harshly.

Jessica paled. 'No!'

'No?' he derided angrily. 'I hope not,' he ground out. 'Because I don't intend for you to *adjust* to my lovemaking, I intend for you to know and want *only* my lovemaking.'

But she was aware over the next few days hat Matthew's lovemaking was a little more restrained, his control intense, his temper volcanic.

She had continued with her job, although Matthew had made it clear that it had to stop once they were married. Not that she minded that. A lot of her near neighbours shopped in the supermaket, and they often chatted to her as she checked their items through. Janet Carter, one of the women from the bus, was one of the more persistent ones on the subject of her and Matthew.

'Was that Mr Sinclair's car I saw outside your house again last night?' she asked as she stood beside Jessica's till.

Jessica kept her head down, concentrating unnecessarily on the price ticket on a packet of biscuits. 'Yesterday evening,' she corrected stiffly, knowing how distinctive the gold Rolls was.

'Same difference,' Janet sniffed; she was a woman in her mid-thirties, having a couple of children of Penny's age, and one of her daughters was actually in Penny's class at school.

'Not at all,' Jessica looked up coolly. 'Night implies that he stayed until morning, whereas evening means we spent a few hours together. It may have escaped your notice,' although she doubted anything escaped this vindictive woman's notice!—'but Mr Sinclair left shortly after eleven.'

'Did he?' the other woman taunted derisively.

'Yes!' Jessica slammed a tin down.

Janet shrugged. 'I can't say I noticed.'

'Well, I'm telling you that he did,' Jessica said tightly, wondering why she was bothering with this woman. Janet Carter would only believe what she wanted to believe in the end.

'No need to get heated,' Janet said with satisfaction, her expression almost smug. 'He's been round a lot lately, hasn't he?'

Jessica gave up all pretence of not being affected by this cross-examination, and glared up at the other woman. 'So?'

'Nothing,' Janet smiled coyly.

'Really?' she said with controlled anger.

The other woman began packing her shopping in her bag. 'Well, it's none of my business what you do——'

'I couldn't agree more!'

'Whatever gets you through the night, that's what I say. And after Andrew I'm sure you need something. Matthew Sinclair must be so much more enjoyable than a sleeping tablet!'

A red tide of anger passed in front of Jessica's eyes. This woman really was a vicious cat!

'Of course, everyone has noticed how—friendly the two of you are,' Janet continued tauntingly. 'Quite the talk of the neighbourhood, you are.'

'Indeed?' Jessica said icily.

'Oh yes. Of course, you would be a fool to turn down the attentions of a man like Matthew Sinclair—but then you haven't, have you?' Janet added with a knowing smile.

Jessica could see the manager of the shop looking in their direction, obviously noticing the fact that the two of them had been in conversation some minutes now. Not that there was anyone else waiting to be served at her till, but chatting to the customers unnecessarily wasn't encouraged.

But Jessica was beyond caring what Alf Young thought at that moment, wanting only to wipe that look of satisfaction off Janet Carter's face. 'No, I haven't,' she answered with false sweetness. 'As you say, I would be a fool.'

'He must make a wonderful—friend.' Janet's eager look invited confidences.

As if she would ever tell this woman anything—anything of such a private nature anyway! 'Oh, he does,' she handed the other woman her bill. 'And I'm sure he'll make an even better husband.' She looked up challengingly.

'H-husband?' Janet faltered, two bright spots of colour in her otherwise pale cheeks. 'Did you say—husband?'

'Yes,' Jessica gave a saccharine-sweet smile. 'Matthew and I are to be married next month.'

'You are?' the other woman gasped. 'I mean—you are?' She sounded incredulous.

'Yes, we are,' Jessica replied with a calmness she was far from feeling.

'Well, I—Congratulations,' Janet said jerkily. 'I had no idea . . .! Peg hasn't mentioned it,' she added almost accusingly.

Jessica had told Peg of her future marriage to Matthew on the night she returned from his house, had known that her friend wouldn't tell anyone—least of all this woman. But Janet Carter's insults had been too much to bear this morning! 'Peg is a dear and trusted friend,' she said pointedly.

'I see.' Janet stiffened.

Jessica doubted it; this type of person only saw what she wanted to see. And now she had revealed the fact of her forthcoming marriage to Matthew she felt deflated, too weary to cross swords with this woman any longer.

Luckily Janet no longer seemed interested in taunting her, hastily paying her bill and leaving the shop. Jessica sat in numbed silence, no longer aware of her surroundings. By tacit agreement she and Matthew had decided not to tell anyone of their wedding until after the fact, and she had no idea how Matthew would react to her having told the biggest gossip in town. Oh dear, she was probably out telling her cronies already!

'Mrs Baxter!' a flustered Alf Young stood in front of her. 'Mrs Baxter, you have a customer.' He looked awkwardly at the woman waiting to pay for her grocieres. 'I'm sorry about this. I don't know what——'

'Excuse me!' Jessica stood up noisily, pushing past the startled couple to run to the staff room.

She was already in her jacket ready to leave when Alf slammed into the room.

'Mrs Baxter, you——' His anger seemed to delate when he saw she was preparing to leave. 'What are you doing? It's only twelve-thirty——'

'I can't work here any more,' she told him jerkily, picking up her bag.

'You mean you're feeling ill——'

'No, I mean I'm leaving. I'm sorry. Of course, I'll forfeit my pay.' She walked to the door. 'I really am sorry.'

'But—but——'

'Please understand, I have to leave,' Jessica choked before runing out of the shop.

She walked in the park for over an hour, wondering what Matthew was going to say about the fact that she had told Janet about them. He would probably be furiously angry, and he had a right to be. What a mess!

She was too distressed to wonder about her concern for Matthew's feelings, too caught up in her already agonised thoughts. The fact that she had walked out on the job that had seemed so important a few months ago didn't touch her at all. Only Matthew mattered, and what he was going to say to her. It would be too much to hope that he wouldn't find out, half the town probably knew already! And it wouldn't be too long before it got back to Matthew . . .

'Jessica, what the hell are you doing?'

She turned with a start at the sound of his voice, forgetting all about the ducks that had so held her attention seconds earlier, leaning back weakly against the railing that surrounded the pond.

Matthew was dressed for the office, in a three-piece suit in a brown lightweight material, the shirt snowy white, his gleaming gold hair brushed neatly into place. In these clothes he looked totally unlike the man she shared her evenings with, and her trepidation grew.

'Jessica?' he frowned darkly at her silence.

She swallowed hard. 'Matthew,' she said in breathless surprise. 'What are you doing here?' She infused lightness into her voice.

'Looking for you,' he grimaced.

'Shouldn't you be at work?' She remained poised as he moved to her side.

'I was,' he said dryly. 'Until I got back from lunch to be congratulated on our forthcoming marriage, by most of my staff, it seemed.'

Janet *had* been busy!

Matthew frowned. 'And when I tried to talk to you at work your boss told me you'd walked out.' He looked at her questioningly.

'I—It—You see—Oh, Matthew!' and she burst into tears, turning her face into the warm comfort of his chest.

'What the hell——!' With gentle hands he manoeuvred her over to a park bench and pushed her down on to it, his arms coming about her as she continued to cry.

Once she started she couldn't seem to stop, and it was several minutes before she took the proffered handkerchief and dried her face. 'I'm sorry,' she choked. 'It isn't like me to cry.'

'No, it isn't,' he agreed softly, his chest vibrating against her cheek. 'Did someone say something to upset you?' he asked in a steely voice.

'Yes—me,' she revealed angrily. 'I lost my temper and—and told—someone that we were getting married . . .'

'Ah!'

She looked up at him worriedly. 'I didn't mean to. She just goaded me——'

'She?'

Jessica blushed. 'A neighbour.'

'Ah!'

'I wish you wouldn't keep saying that,' she snapped. 'What does it mean—ah?' she said irritably.

Matthew's mouth curved into a smile. 'It means I now understand what happened.'

'You—you do?' She looked at him with widely apprehensive eyes. He didn't look angry, but with this man you never could tell.

'Of course,' he still smiled. 'One of your neighbours—happened to notice the extraordinary amount of time I've been spending at your home, and she added two and two together and made five and a half! When she made her snide little comments to you you retaliated by telling her we're getting married.'

'How did you guess?' she asked miserably.

He shrugged. 'By knowing you.'

Jessica looked at him beneath lowered lashes. He still didn't look angry, but then that didn't mean a lot. She had learnt these last months that Matthew could be adept at hiding his feelings when he wanted to be. 'You aren't angry?' she frowned.

'Not at all.' In fact, he looked totally relaxed, almost as if he were enjoying himself.

'Why aren't you?' she snapped, angry with his lack of reaction. 'Everyone knows now that we're getting married——'

'Good.'

'G-good?' she echoed.

'Yes.' He sighed. 'I haven't enjoyed knowing the fact that people have assumed we're having an affair. I don't enjoy being thought a bastard who takes advantage of a lonely widow.'

'But it was your idea to keep it quiet——'

'Yours,' he corrected softly. 'And like any besotted prospective bridegroom I went along with it. I'm glad that it's now public knowledge that we're going to be married.'

Besotted prospective bridegroom! She knew he was only mocking her, and yet she blushed anyway. The only thing he was besotted about was her body. Then why was he marrying her? her subconscious asked. Why, indeed?

'And as it is now public knowledge,' Matthew drawled softly, 'what do you think the locals will make of your crying in my arms like this?'

They were gaining quite a lot of attention; this was a small town, one or both of them was known to each and every one of the people passing through the park.

Jessica straightened away from him selfconsciously. 'They probably think you're jilting me.'

'Never,' he growled, pulling her back into the circle of his arms. 'And just to prove it . . .' his head bent and his mouth possessed hers.

Jessica was too surprised to move away, and her mouth flowered beneath the probe of his, her head bent back as she gave him complete surrender. After all, what could he possibly do to her in a public park?

Quite a lot, apparently! His mouth moved erotically along the edge of her inner lip, encouraging her to return the caress, their lips and hands making love even if their bodies could not.

This eroticism was a new experience for Jessica, and she could feel the tensing of Matthew's body as he enjoyed her uninhibited lovemaking.

'Witch!' he murmured against her lips.

She was surprised at herself. She had never lost control like that before, and her cheeks coloured with embarrassment now.

'No, don't spoil it,' he murmured as she would have moved away. 'I wish this park would miraculously empty, I've always had this fantasy of making love to you in lush green grass under the sun.'

'Matthew!' Her shock was mirrored in her eyes.

He ignored her outburst. 'Maybe we can try it at the house some time. Would you like that?'

She squirmed in embarrassment. Kissing him was one thing, but actually talking about being made love to by him was something else completely.

'Get used to it, Jessica,' he warned softly as he saw how uncomfortable she looked. 'That's far from the only fantasy I've had about you. It could take a lifetime to fulfil all the fantasies I've had about you this last year.'

Jessica couldn't believe it was a year since that company dance, since the night Andrew had been killed. Somehow the time seemed to have sped by. It was a sure fact that Penny was greatly looking forward to the wedding next month, in fact they had had trouble keeping her quiet about it, and her excitement at having Matthew as her father was almost too much for her.

'You may even have a few fantasies of your own,' Matthew continued softly. 'Unless, of course, you shared them all with Andrew,' he rasped harshly.

'No,' she gasped her dismay, very pale.

'No, you didn't share them with him? Or no, you don't want to talk about him?'

His humour had faded now, as it always did when they spoke of Andrew. His jealousy and hatred of the other man was undeniable. 'Both,' she said abruptly.

'Very well.' He stood up, taking her with him. 'And now that everyone knows we're getting married we may as well go and choose the rings.'

'Rings?' she frowned.

'Yes—rings. Have you got everything?' he asked tersely as she bent to pick up her handbag.

'Yes. What rings?' she persisted.

'Our wedding rings.'

'You're going to wear a ring too?' she gasped.

His eyes were narrowed. 'Do you have any objection to my wearing your ring?'

It had never occurred to her that he would want to. She knew most men shunned the wearing of a ring on their wedding finger, that Andrew had refused to even consider wearing one. At the time she had been hurt, later on she had realised that such a ring was a blatant declaration of married status. And Matthew *wanted* to wear one.

'Do you?' he repeated huskily.

'I just never thought . . . I'd like you to,' she admitted

shyly. He looked pleased by her answer, and some of his anger left him as he guided her over to the Rolls-Royce parked at the side of the road a short distance away.

He turned to her once they were seated inside. 'If you can wear my ring showing you belong to me then I'll be honoured to wear one showing I belong to you,' he told her huskily.

'Oh, Matthew!'

'No, don't start crying again,' he chided ruefully. 'The last time I tried to comfort you we nearly caused a public scandal.'

Yes, they had. And she had to admit, to herself at least, that at that moment she hadn't cared that they were in a park, on view to everyone!

CHAPTER EIGHT

THE day that they exchanged the matching plain gold wedding rings the sun shone down on them brightly, with not a cloud in the sky to mar the beauty of the day.

Penny had danced about excitedly all morning, longing to change into the new blue dress she had for the occasion, although Jessica wouldn't let her put it on until the last moment, sure she was going to dirty it.

Her own dress was ivory lace, and her hair was left loosely about her shoulders, a small lacy cap fastened to its silkiness. She carried yellow roses, and her nervousness increased as Peg and George drove her to the register office; the other couple were to act as their witnesses.

But she needn't have been nervous. Matthew took complete control once they arrived, and within minutes, it seemed, they were husband and wife.

'Never take off my ring,' he murmured as he bent to kiss her at the end of the ceremony.

'Never?' She looked up at him shyly.

'Never,' he said firmly, kissing her lingeringly on the lips once again.

Then the guests were congratulating them; most of them were Matthew's relations. His mother had made a special trip over from her native Sweden to attend the ceremony—and Matthew's blondness was at last explained.

They had a small reception at a local hotel. Jessica's house was already closed up, her own and Penny's things had been moved into Matthew's house the week before, the two of them having stayed with Peg and

George for the last few days. It was to the latter that she went to change into her going-away outfit, a pretty lemon dress and jacket, that gave her a glowing appearance. They were only going to London for the weekend, and Penny was to stay with Peg and George for that short time.

Matthew held Jessica's hand as he drove, his smile intimate. 'I was beginning to think this day would never come round,' he grinned.

The day had come round all too soon for Jessica, and the night was approaching even more rapidly. At least they weren't going to the impersonality of a hotel, but would spend the next two days—and nights—in Matthew's London apartment.

It was a typical bachelor home, completely bare of ornaments or flowers, the furniture ultra-modern, as were the paintings on the walls.

Matthew grimaced as he looked around. 'I lease it furnished,' he explained. 'I never realised before just how awful it is.'

'It isn't awful,' Jessica assured him huskily. 'It's just—just——'

'Exactly,' he chuckled, looking completely at ease for the first time in days. 'Come on,' he took hold of her hand, 'I'll show you the rest of it.'

There were two bedrooms, two adjoining bathrooms, and a really lovely kitchen. And the view of the park from the huge Regency windows was beautiful.

'Not that you'll be using the kitchen much,' he gave her a teasing sideways glance. 'Which bedroom shall we use? I usually take the brown one, but I think the bed is bigger in the other one.'

Colour heightened her cheeks. 'The lemon one, then.'

His mouth twisted. 'That's what I thought you would say.'

They had stopped for dinner on the way here, and as

it was now after ten o'clock, and it had been an undeniably long day, there seemed little choice but to go to bed. A nervous fluttering began in the pit of Jessica's stomach at the thought of the night ahead of them.

'Would you like to use the shower first?' he offered.

'I—Thank you.'

This was turning out so much worse than the wedding night she had spent with Andrew. Then she hadn't known what to expect, or what was expected of her, but tonight she knew, and she trembled at the thought of it.

Matthew was wearing only a black robe when she emerged from their bathroom a short time later, her light blue cotton nightgown reaching down to her ankles. Matthew's eyes darkened as he looked at her, but he said nothing as he went through to the bathroom.

Jessica's breath left her with a sigh as the door closed, and she began to tidy her clothes away. How could she go through with this? Because she had to; she was Matthew's wife now, had a duty to him even if she didn't love him.

The room was in darkness when Matthew returned a few minutes later. 'What the——!' The dimmed overhead light was turned on, and Matthew stood frowningly in the doorway, a towel draped loosely about his hips, another towel being used to dry his hair. 'Jessica?' He prompted softly.

She looked at him shyly over the top of the sheet. 'Yes?'

'You weren't hoping to fall asleep before I got in here, were you?' he rasped.

'No, of course not. I just—I wasn't—No,' she finished miserably.

He came to sit on the side of the bed, smoothing her hair back on to the pillow, her face completely bare of make-up, giving her an almost childlike appearance. To the man looking down at her she looked completely vulnerable in that moment, and his breath caught in his throat as her small pink tongue-tip moved tentatively to wet her dry lips.

Jessica was just as aware of him, of his tanned bare chest, the dark blond hair that grew over his chest and taut flat stomach, of his strongly muscled arms, and of his hands gentle on her skin.

'Jessica!' he groaned suddenly, his control breaking completely as he gathered her up in his arms. 'Love me, darling,' he pleaded chokingly. 'Let me make love to you!'

It was the first time love had been mentioned between them, and yet Jessica knew it still wasn't an emotional love he demanded but a physical one. And for her that was even more impossible than emotional love. She had loved Andrew but had been unable to give or receive physical pleasure with him. What chance did a marriage with Matthew, where neither physical or emotional satisfaction existed, have of succeeding?

'The light,' she begged. 'Please turn out the light.'

'Don't be shy,' he smiled encouragingly. 'Let me look at you.' He gently eased the nightgown down her shoulders, his gaze heated as her breasts were bared to him. 'Lord knows you have nothing to be ashamed of,' he groaned, his head lowering as his mouth took possession of one rosy peaked nipple.

Jessica stiffened at the touch of his lips and tongue. Andrew had never liked to touch her breasts, had rarely spared time for the preliminaries, and except when she had breast-fed Penny her breasts had never been touched by another person. Matthew seemed intent on touching and knowing every inch of her, and some of the intimacies he subjected her to made her squirm with embarrassment.

'I like to be touched too,' he taunted softly. The two

of them were naked now, Matthew's hair-roughened skin abrasive against her satiny flesh, her own limbs looking very white against his all-over tan.

'I—I don't——'

He was guiding her hands down his body, every hard muscle and sinew knowing his touch, his ecstatic shudders telling her how deeply he was affected by her caresses.

She was grateful for his teaching, having no idea how she should touch him. Andrew had always seemed to get his pleasure from subjugating her, from knowing she merely suffered his touch, whereas Matthew wanted the pleasure of knowing her body and having her know his in return.

By the time she felt the surging demand of his thighs on hers she knew Matthew's body as well as she knew her own—better; each of his pleasure-spots was known to her, whereas she didn't seem to have any, enjoying the fact that he was liking her body, but knowing none of the physical pleasure herself.

'Are you ready for me, darling?' Matthew groaned into her throat, his body moving slowly against hers. 'I can't wait much longer and I—I can't wait at all!' he moaned heatedly, shuddering in long groans of pleasure as wave upon wave of ecstasy touched him.

Jessica clutched him to her, her nails digging into the taut flesh of his shoulders as she felt him shoot out of control, tears coming unbidden as once again physical pleasure eluded her.

Matthew breathed heavily about her, taking several minutes to attain command of his speech, finally moving from her, taking her with him, her head resting on his shoulder. 'I rushed you,' he murmured regretfully. 'I'm sorry, darling. Next time I'll be more patient. I've just waited so damned long for you,' he added ruefully. 'The feel of you drives me insane!'

They slept for a while, then Jessica came awake to the feel of hands on her body, and her relaxation at once left her, tension taking over as Matthew began to murmur in her ear, those gentle caresses continuing.

Once again she knew only the joy of knowing Matthew had found pleasure within her, although he caressed her heatedly for long timeless minutes before possessing her with an apologetic groan, soon moaning his satisfaction.

Jessica found a certain satisfaction of her own in knowing that Matthew had the release that eluded her, and despite her own frigidity she felt happiness in his caresses, in the gentle love he showed her.

She faced him shyly over the breakfast table, pouring the coffee she knew he liked in the morning. Matthew eyed her guardedly, and some of her happiness in the day faded.

'What would you like to do today?' he asked, having showered and dressed in black cords and a black silk shirt, although Jessica wore only her nightgown and robe, having quietly left the bedroom to prepare the breakfast while Matthew slept on.

'I don't mind,' she shrugged, sensing a reserve in his manner that hadn't been there yesterday. 'What would you like to do?'

'As little as possible!'

'Then we'll stay here,' she smiled as he stretched lazily.

'I have tickets for the theatre tonight, the new Tim Rice and Andrew Lloyd-Webber musical.'

Her face lit up with pleasure. 'That will be lovely!' It had been years since she had been to the theatre.

In the end they spent the day at the apartment, talking easily together—although certainly nothing like a couple on their honeymoon!—going out for an early dinner before continuing on to the theatre.

This time when they retired to the bedroom Jessica didn't feel nervous, knowing that Matthew would show her only gentleness and passion. Once again she felt that happy glow as she later lay in his arms, the movement of his chest beneath her cheek slowly steadying.

But he hadn't fallen asleep this time, she could feel his gaze on her in the darkness.

'What is it?' she asked tremulously.

'How am I failing you?' he said throatily.

Jessica raised her head to look at him. 'Failing me?'

He sighed. 'It isn't good for you like it is for me——'

She put her fingertips over his lips. It was happening too soon! With Andrew it had taken several months for him to start these accusations, for him to realise she was cold towards him. Matthew was so much more experienced, she knew that after only two days of marriage, so maybe he had been able to discern her inadequacies all that much sooner.

'I don't mind——'

'Well, I do!' He sprang out of bed, pulling on his robe. 'You can't forget Baxter, is that it?'

She would never forget Andrew, or the truth he had shown her about herself; it would be useless to say she could. Being with Matthew had only shown her that she was indeed frigid.

'I told you I wasn't much of a bargain,' she choked. 'I told you that at the beginning.'

He flinched as if she had hit him, pale beneath his tan. 'You're my wife, Jessica. And you'll remain my wife!'

It wasn't a good start to any marriage, and she felt relieved when they went back home. At least she would have Penny to relieve the tension between them.

Penny was enthralled to have two attentive parents, seeming to blossom overnight, both socially and scholastically. Her circle of friends doubled, and she was doing so well at school at the end of the year that she came top of her class.

'Clever girl,' Matthew praised once he had seen the letter from her teacher saying how well she was doing.

Jessica would have welcomed such words of praise from him herself. They had been married over a month now, and she would be a fool if she said things were all right between them. They shared a bed, Matthew even made silent love to her every night as if driven to it, but during the day they were like polite strangers sharing a house.

'Are you coming to the meeting with Mummy tomorrow?' Penny was curled happily on Matthew's knee, snuggled into his throat.

Matthew looked at Jessica with narrowed tawny eyes before returning his attention to the small replica of her sitting on his knee. 'What meeting is that, poppet?' he asked softly.

'It's at the school,' she explained excitedly. 'You can see the work I've done the last year.'

'Oh, have you done any?' he teased. 'I thought you'd been too busy flirting with your boy-friend.'

'Don't be silly,' Penny giggled her delight.

'Then who's that young man who always saves you a seat on the schoolbus?'

'Oh, that's only Tony. He's silly,' she wrinkled her nose.

Everything was 'silly' at the moment, and Jessica smiled conspiratorially at Matthew. About her daughter they were in complete accord, both adoring her.

'Poor Tony,' he murmured.

'*Will* you come to the school tomorrow?' Penny persisted.

'We'll see.' He gently pushed her to the ground. 'Go and get ready for your bath.'

Matthew had taken over this nightly ritual as soon as they returned from their honeymoon, bathing Penny while she prepared their dinner, Penny having eaten when she returned from school. When Jessica had protested that he must be tired he had denied it, claiming it gave him time to be with his daughter, having been at work until six or six-thirty.

He waited until Penny had left the room before standing to look down at Jessica. 'Why wasn't I told about this meeting at the school?' he rasped.

She shrugged. 'I didn't think you would be interested.'

'Why not?'

'Well, it's only to meet Penny's teachers and look at her school work. I didn't think you——'

'Would be interested,' he finished grimly.

'Well, I—No,' she sighed. 'I didn't think you would be. It's only for about an hour, and there'll only be—'

'Other parents there. Because I'm Penny's father now,' he told her harshly. 'I may not count as a husband to you, but I am Penny's father!'

'Matthew——'

'Excuse me,' he thrust open the door, 'I have to bathe Penny.' The door closed behind him with controlled force.

Jessica choked back the tears, biting her lip painfully. She had known of the meeting at Penny's school for weeks now, and it seriously hadn't occurred to her that Matthew would want to go. For one thing it was at three-thirty, and Matthew rarely got home before six. For another Andrew had paid little attention to Penny's schooling, and out of habit she hadn't mentioned it to her new husband.

She was in the middle of cooking dinner when Penny came into the kitchen, her face glowingly clean, her damp hair brushed back from her face.

‘’Night, Mummy.’ She reached up to kiss her on the mouth as Jessica stooped down.

‘’Night, darling.’ Jessica hugged her, very conscious of Matthew standing just inside the room, his gaze glowering.

‘I’ll read her a story and then be back with you,’ he told her softly. ‘Can dinner wait that long?’

‘Yes,’ she nodded, not quite able to meet his gaze after their minor argument earlier.

‘What is it?’ Penny sniffed appreciatively.

‘Pork,’ she smiled at her young daughter.

‘Mmm!’ Penny licked her lips.

‘You can have some tomorrow,’ Jessica promised with a laugh.

Penny’s hand was confidently in Matthew’s as they left the room together, and Jessica had to once again blink back the tears as she turned back to the cooker. She had felt tearful a lot lately, often over the silliest things, and it really upset her now that she and Matthew had argued so stupidly.

He was silent during dinner, murmuring appreciation of the meal she had cooked, then carrying his coffee through to the lounge.

He relaxed in an armchair, a record playing softly in the background, the room lit by several lamps placed about the mellow room. ‘So what time is this meeting tomorrow?’ he asked suddenly.

‘Straight after school, at three-thirty. That was—another reason. I didn’t think you would be able to go.’ She sat stiffly on the edge of the sofa, feeling thoroughly miserable. Things had been strained between Matthew and her since their marriage, but they had never actually argued before.

‘I can always make time for Penny,’ he rasped.

‘Oh. I’m sorry—I didn’t realise.’

He looked down at her bowed head, then his expression seemed to soften, he stood up to sit next to her, his arm going companionably about her shoulders. 'If you meet me at the office we could travel to the school together,' he suggested softly, all anger gone now.

Jessica turned to look at him, wondering if she would never get over the fact that this vitally attractive man was now her husband. Just to look at him made her heart beat faster. 'The office?' she faltered.

'Why not? It would save time, and—Lisa!' he realised suddenly, his anger returning with a vengeance. 'Is that it, Jessica? You don't want to face Lisa?' he rasped.

'You don't understand——'

'I understand only too well.' He moved away from her, his expression grim. 'She was your husband's mistress——'

'Yours too,' she reminded him heatedly, an embarrassed flush to her cheeks.

Matthew stood up, his movements impatient. 'My relationship with Lisa can hardly be called that of lover and mistress. We only slept together half a dozen times, usually when I took her away on business with me. And I don't kid myself that your jealousy is on my behalf, you just can't forget that Andrew was with her when he died!' he accused cruelly.

'No——'

'Yes!' he said forcibly, striding over to the door.

'Where are you going?' She looked at him with apprehensive eyes.

'Out!'

'I—Where?' she gulped.

Matthew's mouth twisted. 'Maybe I'll go and see Lisa. As I remember, she was always glad of my—company.'

His words were meant to wound—and they did.

Jessica gave a pained cry, her face buried in her hands as she sobbed. How could Matthew be so cruel, how could he! And would he really go to Lisa Barry?

It was this last thought that sobered her. If he did go to the other woman what would it matter to her? She hadn't cared that Andrew had other women, so why should it bother her if Matthew did the same? It wouldn't, of course it wouldn't. Except that she had come to like and respect him the last few weeks, to *trust* him. So much for that trust now!

She went to the kitchen and tidied up, then went upstairs to check on Penny, finding her daughter fast asleep, her beloved Teddy tucked up in bed with her, although not clutched tightly to her as it had been in the months after Andrew's death. Penny had learnt to trust Matthew too, she had also learnt to love him. Jessica could only hope that his anger with her wouldn't make him do anything to destroy things for her vulnerable daughter.

She went up to bed shortly after ten. But Matthew still hadn't returned, and she had become used to his presence in the bed with her, to his silent reaching out for her, to finding herself held in his arms in the morning, so sleep eluded her.

When she heard the car in the driveway shortly after twelve she hadn't been to sleep at all, had merely lain in the darkness waiting for Matthew's return. Nevertheless, she turned away from the door as if asleep as she heard him ascending the stairs, a shaft of light falling across the bed as he softly opened the bedroom door.

She forced herself to lie still as Matthew moved quietly about the room preparing for bed, her breathing seeming to stop altogether as he climbed in beside her.

'Come over here,' he invited throatily, showing that he had known she was awake all the time.

She stiffened but didn't move. He smelt vaguely of alcohol, and she knew only too well the nastiness of Andrew's mood when he had been drinking.

'Please, Jessica!'

It was the pleading in his voice that was her undoing, and she turned to him with a sob. 'I didn't mean to be stupid about Li—Alicia,' she hiccupped.

'I didn't go to her, Jessica,' he gently touched her cheek. 'I went to the office, got myself quietly drunk. I didn't go to her, darling,' he repeated as she sobbed. 'I wouldn't do that to you.'

'I've been so stupid,' she choked. 'Of course I'll come to the office tomorrow——'

'No,' he cut in gently, his arms possessive. 'I was being unreasonable about that.'

'No, I was. Oh, Matthew, I didn't mean to drive you away,' she clutched on to his shoulders. 'I didn't mean to!'

'Of course you didn't,' he chided, his warm breath ruffling her hair. 'Forget I ever mentioned Lisa. Let me love you, Jessica!' his body had already hardened to passion. 'Let me show you that you're the only woman I want, the only woman I need.'

Her response to him tonight was more than it had ever been before, wanting to please him, knowing that he liked to feel her heated movements beneath him, the way she urged him on to fulfilment.

He put her head on his shoulder afterwards. 'Go to sleep now.' There was a curious flatness to his voice.

She had failed him again, she knew she had. He wanted more from her, and God help her, she was afraid to tell him she had no more to give!

Penny's chatter got them through breakfast the next morning, the six-year-old seeming unaware of her mother's rather worried glances at Matthew's preoccupation.

'I'll see you later then, Mummy.' She collected her satchel and blazer from the hall cupboard.

'Matthew too,' Jessica nodded.

'Are you really going to come to the school?' Penny ran to him eagerly.

He hugged her, putting down his newspaper to do so. 'I really am,' he smiled.

'Oh, goody!' She almost skipped around the room. 'You'll be there at half past three?'

'We won't be late,' Matthew promised indulgently.

Jessica began to clear the table once she had returned from seeing Penny on to the school bus, pouring herself a cup of coffee to sit opposite Matthew. Not that he seemed aware of her presence, he was once again engrossed in his newspaper.

'What time shall I be at the office?' she interrupted the silence.

He looked up sharply. 'I'll call for you here.'

'I'd rather come to the office,' she said firmly.

'Jessica——'

'What time, Matthew?' She met his gaze unblinkingly.

'You don't have to do this, Jessica.'

'But I do. What time?' she persisted.

'Three-fifteen should be time enough.' He neatly folded his newspaper and put it down on the table, looking very handsome in the three-piece pin-striped suit and snowy white shirt.

'Yes.' She stood up. 'I won't be late.'

Matthew glanced at his wrist-watch. 'I'd better be going.' He stood up too, to go to the study and collect his briefcase.

'Matthew . . .'

He turned at the door, a frown to his brow. 'Yes?'

'I—Nothing. Have a good day,' Jessica said brightly,

wondering what impulse had possessed her to try and persuade him not to go to work today but to spend it with her.

He seemed to hesitate, sensing her uncertainty. 'What are you going to do today?'

She shrugged. 'I may ring Peg and ask her if she'd like to go shopping.'

'Good idea,' he nodded abruptly. 'I'll see you later.'

'Yes,' she agreed dully as the front door closed behind him.

After arranging to meet Peg in town for lunch she busied herself tidying the house. Matthew had wanted to get her a housekeeper when they were first married, but she enjoyed looking after the house, taking care of Matthew and Penny, and she didn't want the intrusion of another woman. Besides, this way she could at least be partly a wife to Matthew. As a housewife she knew she was excellent, it was only as a bed-partner that she failed him. *Only* as a bed-partner? God, how naïve she still was! With a sensual man like Matthew a warm and vibrantly alive woman in his bed was very important.

Peg noticed her paleness as they ate lunch, remarking on it. 'You aren't pregnant, are you?' she teased.

'Heavens, no!' Jessica dismissed scathingly. 'At least—I don't think so,' she added uncertainly.

Peg gave a happy laugh. 'Famous last words!'

'Probably,' she agreed absently. There could be no doubting that sooner or later she was going to become pregnant. Matthew had scorned the use of contraceptives, saying he wanted a family, that he didn't intend for Penny to be an only child for long. 'But it's a bit soon,' she frowned.

'David was born nine months after George and I got married,' Peg smiled.

'Yes, but you and George—No, it's too soon,' Jessica repeated abruptly. She had been going to say that Peg and George loved each other—but what did that have to do with producing a baby? She was being stupid today!

'Keep me informed,' Peg made her promise as they parted, having gone on to the shops from their lunch.

Jessica had been glad of her friend's company to help her forget this impending meeting with Alicia Barry. If the truth were known she had kept herself occupied all day just so that she wouldn't think about the meeting. She hadn't seen the other woman since the night Lisa had told her she intended Andrew divorcing her and then marrying her, making her Penny's mother, since the night Andrew had been killed and Lisa had been so badly injured.

Jessica had dressed with care, in a beige-coloured suit and contrasting brown blouse, the high heels on her sandals giving her added height, and her make-up was light and attractive. Nevertheless, she felt herself tensing as she entered Matthew's outer office, Lisa's office . . .

The other woman looked up from her work as Jessica walked towards her, her eyes narrowing to contemptuous blue slits.

It took all Jessica's control not to falter in the face of that insolent stare. Lisa Barry still hated her, she could clearly see that. 'Is Matthew free yet?' she asked determinedly.

For a moment Lisa didn't answer her, the silence hanging between them like an ominous threat. 'He's in a meeting at the moment,' she finally answered in her cold voice. 'But he should be free by three-fifteen. He's cancelled all his other appointments after then so that he can come with you to the school.'

'I see.' Jessica bit her lip awkwardly. The last thing she had envisaged had been having to wait for Matthew. When she had thought of coming here at all

it had been with her leaving immediately,
when at Matthew's side.

'Perhaps you would like to wait?' Lisa invited abr

'What?' she blinked.

The other woman's mouth twisted derisively. 'Yes, over there,' she taunted.

For the first time Jessica noticed several armchairs to the left of the office, and she blushed at her stupidity. 'Thank you,' she said jerkily, moving to sit down.

The telephone rang, diverting Lisa's attention away from her, giving her chance to study the other woman unobserved. Lisa didn't look as if she had changed much in the last year, still as beautiful, showing no sign of the accident that had almost left her crippled for life.

'Seen enough?' her hard voice rasped into the silence.

Jessica blushed once again. Without her realising it the telephone conversation had come to an end, and Lisa had become aware of her close scrutiny. She didn't bother to answer the other woman's rudeness.

Lisa stood up to walk over to her, very tall and elegant in a black and white striped dress, caught in neatly at her narrow waist with a slender black belt, emphasising the fullness of her breasts, her beauty and sophistication an undisputable fact.

She sat down opposite Jessica, supremely confident, crossing one silky leg over the other. 'How do you like being Mrs Matthew Sinclair?' she drawled.

Jessica was visibly taken aback by such a personal question. 'I—I like it,' she answered in a flustered voice.

Lisa nodded, her eyes hard. 'Any woman would. A little different from being Andrew's wife, hmm?' Her mouth twisted.

'Er—yes.' Jessica swallowed hard, wondering where this conversation as leading to.

Lisa's eyes became pebble-hard. 'You didn't grieve very long for Andrew.'

'I——'

'But then you never loved him, did you?' the other woman rasped. Jessica shook her head. 'That isn't true——'

'Don't lie!' Lisa scorned. 'You didn't love him—but I did,' her eyes glittered with hate as she looked at Jessica. 'I loved him, and I could have made him a much better wife than you ever did. And now he's dead.'

'Alicia——'

'Don't touch me!' she spat the words out, shaking off Jessica's hand on her arm.

Jessica looked down at her hands, not knowing what to do next; what to say to this woman. Lisa had loved Andrew deeply, and there was nothing she could say to that.

Lisa stood up, her hands white where they were clenched together. 'I know he was weak,' she began to talk again, 'that he had his faults—but I loved him!' Her expression was venomous as she looked at Jessica. 'You didn't want him, you only needed a father for your child. You didn't even sleep with him, hadn't done for years.'

Jessica blanched. How could Andrew have discussed such personal details with this woman? She knew the answer to that already. Andrew would have taken great pleasure in relating the details, or lack of them, of their sex-life, to Alicia Barry.

Lisa gave her a scathing glance. 'Matthew doesn't look as if he's doing any better,' she said insultingly.

If anything Jessica paled even more. Surely Matthew hadn't discussed . . .? No, she couldn't believe that of him.

Lisa looked pleased by Jessica's sickly pallor. 'You don't stand a chance of holding Matthew if you don't please him in bed,' she scorned. 'He's a very physical man, one of the unselfish few who like you to enjoy it too. And you don't, do you, Jessica?' she taunted.

'Please——'

'Please!' the other woman echoed shrilly. 'Can you bring Andrew back? Can you *give* him back to me? No, of course you can't!' Her eyes were fevered. 'So why should I let you have Matthew?' she ground out.

Jessica swallowed hard, her eyes huge and haunted. 'Wh-what do you mean?' she choked.

Lisa's expression was contemptuous. 'Matthew will become mine again just like that,' she flicked her finger and thumb together.

Jessica recoiled, wondering why she didn't get up and walk away, why she stayed here and listened to these torturing words.

'Well, have you nothing to say?' the other woman taunted.

Jessica straightened. 'I don't believe you,' she said clearly.

Lisa's mouth curved into a mocking smile. 'Don't you? How unfortunate for you. I only have to say the word . . .' she added pointedly.

'Then why don't you?' Jessica challenged with more confidence than she felt.

'Because I'm not ready to yet,' the other woman said calmly. 'But when I am you'll know about it.'

'Because you'll tell me?' she scorned.

Lisa smiled. 'I won't need to. There will come a night when you'll know that he's mine, when you know that your frigid little body no longer attracts him!'

CHAPTER NINE

WHAT would have been said next Jessica had no idea, for the door to the inner office opened, and Matthew and another man entered Lisa's office. Matthew's narrowed tawny gaze flickered over the two women before his attention returned to the man at his side.

'I'll get my lawyer to look over the contract and get back to you on it next week.' He shook the man's hand warmly.

''Bye, Matthew,' the other man nodded, giving only a cursory glance in Lisa's and Jessica's direction before leaving.

'Darling!' Matthew crossed to Jessica's side, kissing her briefly on the mouth, his eyes once again narrowed at her lack of response. He turned to Lisa, a perfectly composed Lisa now. 'You should have told me my wife was here.' His voice was hard.

Jessica licked her lips nervously at the other woman's insolent stare. 'I—I've only just arrived,' she excused.

'Nevertheless——'

'We should be going, Matthew,' she reminded him, ignoring Lisa's triumphant look.

She didn't need an explanation of that look. If she were sure of Matthew, if they had loved each other, she wouldn't have hesitated about denouncing the other woman's insulting behaviour seconds earlier. By remaining silent she was only confirming what Lisa had already guessed. She knew all that, and yet she couldn't risk testing Matthew's loyalty. With the deterioration of their marriage she had no idea whose side he would take! 'You promised Penny you wouldn't be late,' she said jerkily.

His expression softened at the mention of Penny. 'I'll just get my briefcase,' and he returned to his office.

'So you've trapped another one with your daughter,' Lisa drawled. 'Still, that's no problem,' she dismissed. 'When Matthew divorces you he may be able to get custody of Penny.'

'She's my daughter!'

'Yes—and you aren't fit to be her mother, are you?' Lisa scorned harshly. 'Oh yes, Andrew told me about that too,' she mocked at Jessica's pained gasp. 'Something I'm sure dear Matthew has no idea of.'

'You wouldn't—oh, you wouldn't——'

'You are a mess, aren't you?' Lisa snapped contemptuously. 'No, I won't—not just yet. But I will tell him some time, maybe one night when we're in bed together. Matthew can be very—receptive when he's in bed,' she taunted.

Jessica was grey with shock. 'Alicia——'

'Ready?' Matthew came back into the room, looking at their tense faces enquiringly. 'Anything wrong?' he queried lightly.

Lisa was the first to recover her composure, smiling at him. 'Nothing at all. I was just congratulating Mrs Sinclair. You make a wonderful boss, so you must be a fantastic husband.'

He grinned. 'I hope I am.'

'Oh, Mrs Sinclair assures me you are,' she purred.

Matthew gave Jessica a probing glance, but made no comment, 'We'd better be going, darling,' he said briskly.

Jessica went with him silently, too numb to do more than sit meekly at his side as he drove to Penny's school. Andrew had told Lisa about so much more than just their sex-life—or lack of it, he had told the other woman things that could destroy her life for a second time. And Alicia Barry seemed vindictive enough to use that information—when it suited her to.

'All right?' Matthew prompted softly.

'I—Yes,' she nodded.

'It wasn't so bad, was it?' he said lightly.

She gave him a sharp look. 'What wasn't?'

'Meeting Lisa again.'

Could he really be that dense? Alicia Barry had oozed hatred, and surely Matthew couldn't have missed seeing her own pale face. It seemed he could. But maybe he wanted to. It was bad enough that his home life was so seriously disrupted, without it being strained at the office for him too.

Penny was waiting for them at the door of her classroom, her face lighting up as she saw them. She stood between them to take a hand of each, taking them proudly into the room.

Jessica and Matthew exchanged a look of understanding, Jessica smiling as Mrs Howard, Penny's form teacher of the last year, came to greet them.

'Mrs Baxter!' she beamed.

'She isn't Mrs Baxter any more,' Penny put in knowledgeably. 'This is my new daddy,' she pulled Matthew forward. 'And his name is Sinclair, so Mummy's is too.'

'I see,' Mrs Howard smiled. 'So this is the new daddy you told us all about.'

'Yes,' Penny said proudly, 'I'll go and get my best painting, shall I, Mummy?' she looked up eagerly.

'You do that, darling,' Jessica nodded absently.

'Told you about?' Matthew enquired softly of the teacher.

'Oh yes, Mr Sinclair,' the middle-aged woman smiled. 'The class had to write one sentence about each of their parents, then read it out to the class.

Would you like to see Penny's piece?'

'Well——'

'Daddy, Daddy!' Penny came running back to grasp Matthew's hand. 'Come and meet Tony.'

He gave a rueful smile, his eyebrows raised. 'Asked to meet her boy-friends already!' he said teasingly to the two women before he was dragged away, although there was an emotional catch in his voice as he spoke.

Mrs Howard's expression softened as she watched them, then she turned to find Jessica blinking back the tears. 'The first time Penny has ever called Mr Sinclair Daddy?' she enquired gently.

'Yes,' she choked.

'She loves him.'

'Yes.'

'That much was obvious from what she wrote about him. I'll show it to you.' The teacher went to her desk and brought forward the notebook.

It was only two lines, for Penny didn't really write very well yet, but it was enough to tell Jessica how deeply her daughter loved Matthew. 'I love Mummy very much. I love my new daddy much more than my old one.'

She slowly closed the book, looking across the room to where Matthew was down on his haunches talking to Penny and Tony, making the two children giggle. Yes, she liked Penny's 'new daddy' better than the 'old one' too.

Matthew took a couple of weeks off during Penny's summer holidays, and the three of them went to the coast together. For Jessica it was a time of really getting to know her husband, and he was more relaxed too, the two of them at least having a relaxed camaraderie by the time they returned home.

But nothing else had changed for them. Matthew still reached for her in the night, his lovemaking silent and restrained, almost as if he took her against his will. Jessica gave him all the warmth that she could, but she knew it still wasn't enough for Matthew. And it was no longer enough for her either. She hungered for fulfilment, ached with a desire she knew could never be. And Matthew seemed to sense her tension.

'What is it?' he asked one evening as they sat down after dinner, Penny tucked snugly up in bed. 'You seem—restless.'

'It's the passing of summer,' she dismissed, looking up from her sewing.

'It's only September,' he teased.

'I've never liked winter,' she evaded, knowing their own strained relationship was the main reason for her unrest.

'Would you like to go out one evening?'

'Go out?' she frowned. 'But Penny——'

'Would be all right for one evening, surely. I'm sure Peg would baby-sit for us. Penny seems secure enough now, don't you think?' he added softly.

Jessica blinked to hide her confusion. 'I don't know what you mean.'

'I read what Penny wrote too, Jessica,' he said gently. 'She came across as a very insecure little girl. I had no idea she felt that way about Andrew.'

Neither had she. She had been deeply affected by what Penny had written, and she had tried to stop Matthew seeing it. As usual he had been determined, reading the two sentences without a word. In fact, he hadn't spoken about it until tonight.

'Maybe she's still angry with him because he left her—children don't understand these things.'

'You think that's all it was?' he frowned.

'I'm sure of it.'

He nodded. '*Would* you like to go out for an evening? Say, tomorrow?'

'I don't——'

'I'd like it, Jessica.'

Of course he would, and she was being selfish. Until he had met her, when he was still spending most of his time in London, he had probably had a full social life. Strangely the two of them had only ever been out together for an evening on their honeymoon, probably because of the strangeness of their courtship. But that was no reason for them not to go out, and as Matthew said, Peg would baby-sit for them, in fact she had already offered to several times and Jessica had refused.

'I'd like it too,' she smiled shyly.

'Good.' He looked pleased, less strained himself. 'I'll make the arrangements.'

Penny didn't make a murmur when told she was to be left with Aunt Peg for the evening, and she went off to bed quite happily at her usual time.

'She's a different child.' Peg watched the little girl go upstairs with Matthew.

'Yes.' There was an emotional catch in Jessica's voice. She had noticed the difference in her daughter too, the spontaneity, the happiness she radiated.

'I wish the same could be said for you.' Peg looked at her critically. 'You don't look well, Jessica.'

'I feel fine,' she dismissed.

'Do you?'

'Yes!' she bit her bottom lip. 'I'm sorry, Peg, I didn't mean to shout.'

'That's all right, love.' Her friend squeezed her hand understandingly. 'But both you and Matthew look a little—peaked.'

Jessica shrugged. 'Every marriage has its teething problems.'

'Yes. But——'

'Ready, darling?' Matthew came back into the lounge, his eyes darkening appreciatively. 'You look as if you are. You look beautiful,' he told her huskily.

Jessica blushed at his compliment, catching Peg's pleased expression before quickly looking away again. Peg had obviously made the comparison she had, remembering Andrew's lack of interest in her appearance the night of the Company dance and comparing it unfavourably with Matthew's genuine pleasure in her appearance. She didn't need the comparison to know that her husband was a better man than Andrew could ever have been.

She had taken special care with her appearance tonight, had bought a new dress in soft red shades, knowing the brightness of the colour added to the glow of her cheeks, deepening the colour of her eyes.

'So do you—look handsome, I mean.' She blushed at her awkwardness, knowing that any woman would be proud to be seen in Matthew's company, his rugged good looks complemented by the brown velvet jacket, snowy white shirt, and brown trousers he wore. He was enough to set any woman's pulse racing; he had so much more than mere good looks, he had a magnetism that was sensual.

He wrote a telephone number down on the pad next to the telephone. 'The restaurant, in case you should need us,' he told Peg. 'I'd better get Jessica out of the house before she gives me any more compliments and I decide I'd rather stay at home!' He gave a mischievous grin.

Peg laughed, waving at them from the open doorway as they drove off.

Jessica was still blushing from the implication Matthew had made in front of her friend. 'Did you have to do that?' she said stiffly.

'Do what?' He glanced at her absently.

'Make Peg think that we—that you——'

'That I desire you,' he finished grimly. 'But I do.'

'I know that.' The colour seemed to be a permanent fixture in her cheeks. 'I just wish you hadn't—that you hadn't given the impression——'

'Don't worry, Jessica,' he rasped. 'All newly married couples do it—old married ones too if they get the chance.'

'I didn't mean that. I meant—Oh, what do I mean?'

'I have no idea,' he said in a weary voice. 'Let's just forget it, Jessica. It was said as a joke, and I'm sure Peg took it as such.'

So was she, and she felt stupid for making such an issue of it. She had probably ruined the whole evening now.

Matthew didn't give the impression that she had, and his arm was about her waist as they were shown to their table in the most exclusive restaurant in the area, his manner solicitous as they ate their meal.

And yet she was aware that his attitude towards her had changed since they were married, that his eyes no longer looked at her warmly but guardedly, that he no longer demanded or coaxed her response when he made love to her but had accepted her coldness. And she dreaded the final breakdown of their marriage, at least feeling she was giving Matthew something in return while she shared his bed.

'Penny for them?' he prompted softly, the candlelight flickering on the table between them, muted music muffling the conversation of their fellow-diners. 'One new penny,' he clarified smilingly.

Jessica looked up at him uncertainly, seeing no cynicism in his expression. 'I was just thinking what a nice restaurant this is.'

Matthew sat back in his chair, sipping the red wine they had drunk with their meal. 'You've never been here before—with Andrew?'

'No,' she shook her head.

'Where did you go with Andrew?' He was looking down into his wine glass, his expression forbidding.

'Er—Nowhere very much,' she said lightly. 'We had Penny, and——'

'That's no excuse, Jessica,' he rasped. 'I'm sure Peg has always been willing to baby-sit. Besides, Andrew always came over as a man who liked to join in rather than sit at home.'

'He was.' She avoided his gaze. 'But I didn't realise you knew Andrew that well. He was only one of your employees.'

His mouth twisted. 'Andrew was the sort of man who always stood out in a crowd. Besides——' he broke off.

'Besides . . .?' Jessica prompted sharply.

Matthew shrugged. 'He was your husband.'

She shook her head. 'That wasn't what you were going to say.'

'What do you want to hear, Jessica?' he demanded fiercely. 'That he was always in Lisa's office? That for two months before he died it got so that I couldn't go into her office without falling over him? *Is* that what you wanted to hear, Jessica?' His eyes glittered savagely.

'If you're trying to tell me they'd been having an affair for two months before he died then I already knew,' she told him dully.

'How?'

'I just—I knew,' she shrugged.

His mouth twisted contemptuously. 'What happened, did he stop making love to you?'

'No!' she gasped her shock.

A nerve worked erratically in his jawline, his breathing ragged. 'Then how did you know? Did he tell you?'

'No—Penny did.' She turned away. 'Now could we please leave?'

'Yes!' He stood up noisily, his face stony as they left the restaurant to get into the waiting car. 'Explain that remark about Penny,' he bit out.

She absently watched the headlights of the cars going in the other direction. 'Why do you need to know?' she sighed at last. 'It happened before I met you.'

'If it involves Penny then it concerns me,' he said grimly. 'She's my daughter now, and I want to know about anything that may have disturbed her.'

'Disturbed her? But——'

'Upset her, then,' he dismissed impatiently. 'How did she know about Lisa?'

Jessica haltingly explained about the way Andrew had taken Penny shopping with his mistress, knowing that Matthew wouldn't stop until he knew the truth.

'The bastard!' he rasped when she had finished.

'I'm sure Penny didn't realise——'

'I don't mean because of that,' he snapped. 'As you say, I'm sure Penny didn't realise. But what sort of man takes his mistress shopping for his wife's birthday present?'

'Andrew,' she said bitterly.

'No wonder you questioned whether or not I bought the Christmas presents myself.' He shook his head. 'I also chose those earrings and necklace,' he added softly.

Jessica had been taken aback when on their wedding day Matthew had presented her with a jewellery box. Inside had been diamond ear-studs and a matching necklace in gold and diamond links. She was wearing them tonight, the first occasion she had had to do so since their honeymoon.

'I never doubted it,' she told him clearly.

'Thank you.' His hand clasped hers where it rested on her thigh, his warmth detectable through the silkiness of her dress. 'Why didn't you leave him, Jessica? I'm sure there must have been others before Lisa.'

'Dozens,' she confirmed with a bitter laugh.

'Then why—Because you loved him,' he said heavily.

She didn't answer. The real reason she had never left Andrew was because of fear, because of that hold he had over her which Alicia Barry now knew about.

She prepared for bed while Matthew drove Peg home, going in to check on Penny before taking her bath. The scented water helped relax her, but she knew the evening had been far from a success; they had talked about Andrew too much for it to be that. And Andrew was a subject guaranteed to displease Matthew. Maybe if they had a child of their own . . . But a child didn't necessarily bring a couple closer together, she and Andrew had proved that when Penny was born, and Matthew couldn't love Penny more if she *were* his own child. But nevertheless, a child between them would be nice.

She was in bed reading when Matthew returned, although she put her magazine down as he entered the bedroom.

'Penny all right?' he asked as he took off his bow tie and jacket, sitting down on the bed to take off his shoes and socks.

'Fine,' she nodded, watching unashamedly as he undressed, having lost that shyness with him at least. He had a wonderful body, wide-shouldered, a taut flat stomach, strong surging thighs, his legs long and muscular, with not an ounce of unnecessary flesh anywhere.

'Have you showered?' He stood naked in front of her, not in the least selfconscious.

'Bathed.' She knew the reason he asked. They occasionally showered together, and a couple of times Matthew had even made love to her in the shower.

He nodded. 'I won't be long.'

She knew that too, and tonight she welcomed the

taking of her body. She needed that reassurance, that closeness to him; she had felt him slowly fading from her all evening. And if they lost his physical revelling in her body what would they have left?

She turned to him eagerly as he joined her in the bed minutes later, felt his instantaneous response to her nakedness, opening her mouth to his kiss.

'Jessica!' he groaned as she returned the caress, his senses leaping.

'Love me,' she invited. 'Please love me!'

He needed no further encouragement. His kisses were slow and drugging, his caresses knowledgeable, his lips sensual on her hardened nipples, slowly moving down to her thighs, kissing her silken flesh with an emotion akin to worship.

Jessica felt her own surging need, groaning her frustration as she knew, once again, it would be for nothing. It wasn't Matthew's fault, he certainly wasn't a selfish lover, it was just her own frigidity.

'What is it?' Matthew sensed her withdrawal.

She gave him a bright smile. 'Nothing. Darling——'

He rolled back on to his side of the bed, the bed they had shared for the last three months, closing his eyes momentarily before pushing himself up off the bed.

'Matthew . . .?' She looked at him with bewildered eyes.

'I can't stand it any more, Jessica.' He stood with his back towards her, pulling on the bathrobe he had discarded on to the bedroom chair earlier. 'I've tried, God knows I've tried . . .' He buried his face in his hands.

'Matthew!' She was off the bed in seconds, tentatively touching his arm, feeling him flinch.

He spun round, his eyes bloodshot, his face gaunt. 'Don't touch me!' he rasped. 'For God's sake don't touch me!'

She was unknowingly provocative in her nakedness, and she pulled her robe on with shaking hands as Matthew thrust it at her, tying the belt firmly about her waist.

Matthew watched her movements with hooded eyes. 'I can't carry on like this any more, Jessica,' he told her quietly.

She swallowed hard. 'What do you mean?' She felt cold all over, shivering involuntarily.

A pulse beat erratically in his throat. 'I've done my best, for three months I've suffered your coldness towards me in bed, and now I can't take it any more.'

'But, Matthew——'

He moved away from her hand. 'I'm going to sleep in the spare room——'

'No!' she gasped in a choked voice.

'Yes,' he said savagely, his eyes glittering. 'If I stay here I'll make love to you, and if I do that I'll only wake up disgusted with myself once again.'

Jessica was very pale too now. 'Disgusted . . .?'

'I'm making love to a shell,' he rasped harshly. 'You never let me near the real you, the inner you. You save all that for the bastard you still love.'

'Andrew?'

'Yes—Andrew. I'm sick of his bloody name! Go to bed, Jessica,' he sighed heavily. 'I won't be touching you again tonight.' He closed the door with controlled force.

How long she stood there she never knew, only coming to an awareness of her surroundings when her shivering became uncontrollable. She was like ice, both physically and emotionally.

Matthew had already left the house when she and Penny breakfasted the next morning, and she had the difficult task of inventing an excuse for her daughter. It was easy enough to say Matthew had to be at work early, but she didn't like lying to her daughter. She knew the real reason Matthew had left so early had been because he had been avoiding her.

The house got its second complete spring-cleaning in three months that day, all the curtains washed, all the furniture meticulously polished, the whole of the kitchen washed down. And still Jessica had enough energy to do all the washing and ironing, jumping nervously as the telephone began ringing late that afternoon.

'Jessica?'

'Matthew!' she sighed her relief at hearing from him. But what he had to say next dashed any hopes she might have had that he had called so they could make their peace.

'I have to go to London on business for a few days,' he told her distantly. 'Could you pack a suitcase for me so that I'm not delayed leaving?'

'I—Of course. When are you going?' She held the receiver tightly in her hand, her knuckles showing white.

'Straight after work. I'll just stop off and collect my case and then——'

Jessica wasn't listening any more. Matthew was going away. It couldn't just be coincidence that he was going so soon after their argument, he had to be going deliberately. And there was nothing she could do or say to stop him!

'Jessica?' He seemed to have noticed her silence.

'Will you have time to say goodbye to Penny?' she asked stiffly.

'Of course.' He sounded exasperated. 'Look, this trip couldn't be avoided, Jessica.'

'No, I'm sure it couldn't. How long will you be gone—so that I know how much to pack?' she added, in case he should think she was prying into his private business. He had made it obvious last night that he didn't consider her a real wife to him.

'Four or five days, possibly a week. I'd take you with me, but there's Penny's schooling, and I'll probably be working most of the time anyway.'

'I understand.'

Matthew sighed. 'I hope you do. We need time, Jessica, *I* need time.'

'I understand,' she said again.

'Well, I—I'll see you later, then.'

'Yes,' and she rang off.

Suddenly all her energy was sapped from her, and she sank down on to the chair next to the telephone. Matthew was going away—would he come back?

Penny was predictably upset that her daddy was going away, and she said a miserable goodbye to him when he got home.

'It won't be for long, darling,' he assured her gently.

'You'll come back?' she voiced the question Jessica had been frightened to.

He glanced up at her with a frown, seeing only the cool exterior, the calm expression. 'Of course I'll come back.' He turned back to Penny. 'Before you know it.' He tapped her lightly on the nose, then stood up to look at Jessica once again. 'I have to go now.'

'Can't you stay to dinner?' she asked breathlessly, not wanting him to go yet, hating the emotional distance between them and yet not knowing how to bridge it.

'No, I don't have time. Lisa is waiting for me,' he added quietly for her ears alone.

'Lisa . . .?' she swallowed hard.

'Yes,' he confirmed tersely. 'She's outside in the car.' He picked up his suitcase, kissing her briefly on the mouth before turning to leave.

How Jessica managed to stop herself from crying she never knew, but she had to be strong for Penny's sake.

As it was Penny was so upset at Matthew's departure that she was inconsolable.

Jessica finally managed to calm her daughter down, assuring her that Matthew would soon come back to them, that he was probably missing them as much as they were missing him.

The latter she wasn't so sure of. Alicia Barry was with him in London, and he had openly admitted to her that he and Lisa were lovers when they went away on business. Would they be lovers tonight? The thought of that caused a shaft of pain to shoot through her. She couldn't bear it if Matthew betrayed her with the other woman.

The telephone rang just after nine, and she rushed to answer it, desperate not to wake Penny—it had taken her ages to get her to sleep.

When she heard Matthew's voice she didn't know whether to laugh or cry. 'You're all right, aren't you?' she asked worriedly.

'I'm in London,' he confirmed. 'I just wanted to check that Penny was all right.'

Penny? What about her! 'She's asleep,' she assured him huskily.

'Any problems?'

She could be his housekeeper for all the personal interest he took in her! 'Penny was a little upset, but she's fine now,' she assured him in the same cool tones as he was using.

'Good,' he said briskly. 'I'll give you the number of my office and flat, in case you need me. I forgot earlier.'

Because he had been so desperate to escape! And Jessica knew, no matter what the situation, that she couldn't call Matthew on either of these numbers. She would be too frightened Lisa Barry might answer.

As she lay in her lonely bed later that night she had to accept the real reason she was so afraid of Alicia

Barry. She had taken one husband from her, a man she had feared and hated, but if she took Matthew from her too she would be taking the man Jessica loved. She *loved* Matthew Sinclair!

CHAPTER TEN

How could she have deceived herself—and Matthew—all these months! She wasn't frightened of him, was no longer indifferent to him—if she ever had been. She loved her husband, loved him with an intensity that made her long to tell him of her feelings, even if he should reject her. He had always given her honesty, embarrassingly so at times, and she would give him the same honesty. She loved him, *loved* him.

It made her feel incredibly alive; her senses were singing, just longing for his return. If he gave her a second chance she would—Would what? Didn't she still have that fault in her fundamental make-up? That hadn't changed, loving Matthew couldn't do that for her; she had loved Andrew when they were first married, and it had made no difference then. But it had been a different kind of love, she could see that. She had loved Andrew with an adolescent love, a child's love; she loved Matthew with every adult emotion in her body.

When he called late on Friday afternoon to tell her he would be home the next day her emotions were mixed. She longed to see him again, and yet she feared what he might say on his return. What if his 'time' had convinced him that their marriage couldn't continue—with more than a little help from Alicia Barry?

His manner when he arrived home told her nothing of his thoughts or feelings, and he looked very tired, as if the last week had been a great strain to him.

Penny was very excited to have him back, launching herself into his arms, showing none of the restraint that

Jessica had when she had kissed him shyly on the cheek seconds earlier.

She looked at him with new eyes now, through the eyes of a woman in love, and she could see him for the incredibly handsome man he was, the raw sensuality in his tawny eyes that burnt like a flame. He was dressed casually for travelling, in black slacks and a light blue shirt, that added to his air of rugged attraction.

'Mummy's made a special dinner,' Penny told him proudly. 'She's been in the kitchen *all* afternoon.'

'Not quite,' Jessica denied awkwardly, wondering if she shouldn't teach her daughter a little more discretion. She had spent a couple of hours in the kitchen making an elaborate chicken dish and a gateau for dessert, but it was a little disconcerting when your young daughter let out your secrets.

Matthew gave her a sympathetic glance, swinging Penny up into his arms as he stood up. 'Then I'd better give you your present so you can get to bed and let us eat this delicious dinner.'

Penny was enchanted with her Beefeater doll, putting it in pride of position on her dressing-table, raising no objections when she was put to bed a short time later, although she clung to Matthew as he kissed her goodnight. 'You won't go away again?' She looked up at him, looking very like Jessica in that moment.

'No,' he assured her huskily, smoothing back her hair. 'I'll never leave you again. If I have to go away again I'll take you with me. I missed you too much to leave you behind.'

Jessica turned away, blinking back the tears as she went down to put the finishing touches to their meal.

Matthew had showered and changed when he joined her a few minutes later, his hair still damp, his body smelling of some sort of tangy aftershave or cologne, his fresh clothing still casual, brown trousers and a cream shirt.

Jessica placed the start of their meal in front of him, a pâté she knew he particularly liked. 'Did you mean it?' she asked huskily as she sat opposite him.

He frowned. 'Mean what?' His manner had been cool since he got home, and his distant tone now was no more encouraging.

'That you won't be leaving Penny—and me—again?'

His glance was probing. 'Would you care?'

'You know I——'

'No, Jessica,' he sighed. 'I don't know anything about you. And unless you want to ruin this delicious dinner I suggest you leave this discussion until after we've eaten.'

For Jessica the meal was already ruined. 'This discussion' sounded so ominous, as if Matthew had indeed come to some important decisions while he had been away.

By the time she had cleared away the debris from their meal she was so tense she was at screaming pitch. Neither of them had done justice to the meal, their conversation had been stilted.

'Penny is asleep,' he told her when she came back from the kitchen.

She nodded. 'Did—did your business go well in London?'

He sighed, studying the brandy in the bottom of his glass. 'There was no business in London—but then you knew that, didn't you?' he looked at her in challenge.

'I—I guessed,' she nodded.

'Yes,' he said dully. 'Sit down, Jessica. I think we should have that talk now.'

She sat heavily, very pale, sitting primly on the edge of the chair. What Matthew had to say next could change her whole life.

He seemed to be gathering his thoughts together,

choosing his words carefully. 'I had to get away,' he spoke slowly. 'From you. Oh, not for the reason you're thinking,' he added as she flinched. He put a hand up over his eyes. 'You must know by now the physical effect you have on me.'

'Yes.'

'And the lack of physical effect I have on you,' he sighed.

Jessica swallowed hard. 'Yes.'

'I don't enjoy forcing myself on you——'

'Oh, you don't——'

'Let's not delude ourselves, Jessica,' he smiled without humour. 'When we're in bed together I make all the moves, never once have you turned to me.'

It was true; she always waited for him to make the first move, never encouraged his advances.

'I could try——'

'Don't you understand I don't want you to *try*,' Matthew cut in impatiently. 'Love shouldn't be *tried* at, it should just happen, because you both want it.' He stood up to pace the room. 'You merely *suffer* my touch——'

'No!'

'Yes,' he insisted dully. 'And each time it happens, each time I'm driven to making love to you, I lose a little more self-respect.' He gazed down at her steadily. 'I shall be sleeping in the spare room from now on.'

'No!' she gave a wounded cry.

'Yes, Jessica,' he sighed. 'Until we sort ourselves out I have to stay away from you.'

'But I—Are you leaving me, Matthew?' she choked.

'Hell, no,' he dismissed scathingly. 'I couldn't leave you even if you actually hated me. And you don't hate me, do you, Jessica?'

'No,' she admitted softly.

'But you don't love me either.' He turned away.

'I——'

'No false declarations, Jessica,' he said impatiently. 'That I couldn't stand.'

'But I——'

'I couldn't stand it!' he repeated grimly. 'I'm going to bed,' he put his glass down. 'It's been a long week.'

'Matthew!' Her frantic cry stopped him at the door.

'Yes?' his tone wasn't encouraging.

'I—I—Nothing,' she muttered. 'Goodnight.'

He nodded abruptly before leaving, his footsteps heavy on the stairs.

It was no good chastising herself, although she did so anyway. She had had the perfect opportunity to tell him of her realised love for him, and yet years of hiding her true feelings had made it impossible to voice her love for Matthew.

She could hear him in the bathroom as she passed it on her way to the master bedroom, could hear the shower running. She couldn't let him sleep in the spare bedroom, knew that sort of arrangement could never come to an end. Matthew had said she never made the first move—well, tonight she was going to, she was going to go to him and tell him how she felt.

She removed all her clothes before entering the bathroom, where Matthew was in the process of drying himself, although his movements stopped dead as soon as he saw her, his breath being released in a hiss as she pressed her nakedness against his.

'I've made the first move, Matthew,' she told him softly. 'In fact, I'll make all the moves, if you'll let me.'

His heart was beating heavily and fast. 'I don't understand . . .'

Jessica swallowed hard, knowing she had to tell him the truth. 'I love you,' she murmured. 'I love you, Matthew.'

His hands grasped her arms painfully as he held

her away from him. 'Jessica . . .?'

'Don't say anything, darling,' she groaned. 'Just love me.'

His mouth covered hers, his body moving druggingly against her, his hands shaking as he caressed her. His eyes glittered as he raised his head. 'Do you really mean it?' he moaned. 'Do you love me?'

'Yes,' she replied unflinchingly.

'I love you too!' He buried his face in her throat, just holding her, letting their mutual love wash over them. 'I've loved you from the moment I saw you,' he murmured against her silken hair. 'I would have taken you off and married you then if you hadn't already got a——'

'Not tonight, darling,' she put her fingertips over his lips to silence any talk of Andrew. 'Let's just think about us,' she said huskily, a warm glow about her as she accepted the precious gift of his love. 'Just you and me.'

'Yes,' he smiled, the strain leaving him. 'I like the sound of that.' He bent down and swung her up in his arms.

'What are you doing?' she gasped.

'Taking you to our bedroom,' he said with satisfaction. 'I can hardly make love to you on the bathroom floor, my love,' he teased.

Once in their bed Jessica responded mindlessly, giving herself completely into her husband's tender care, holding nothing back from him, giving him all of her love, all of herself, racked with surprise—and exultation, as she felt a warm burning pleasure filling her body, every single particle, from her head to her heels, down to her very fingertips, taking her higher and higher——

'Give it to me, darling,' Matthew choked, his body joined with hers, their thighs moving to an erotic rhythm. 'Give it all to me!'

She had no idea what he meant, had no idea what this wild excitement was all about. And then suddenly she knew, knew with startling clarity. Wave after wave of ecstasy possessed her body, an ecstasy that Matthew controlled to the glorious end, only taking his own breathless pleasure when he was sure Jessica had fulfilled all her passion.

'Thank you,' he kissed her face and throat with heated lips. 'Thank you!' he groaned, his arms tight about her, their bodies still joined together.

Jessica was still so shaken she couldn't speak. She wasn't frigid, had never been frigid!

'Oh, Matthew!' she hugged him tearfully. 'Matthew!' She glowed up at him, sure that she had never felt so happy in her life, feeling a satisfaction that went into her bones.

'I know,' he gave a choked laugh too. 'I never knew making love could be so beautiful,' he breathed huskily. 'So absolutely beautiful,' and his arms tightened convulsively.

'Yes,' she buried her face against his damp salty skin, 'it was.' She had never dreamt it could be like this, that loving someone could give so much pleasure. She had been married before, had an almost seven-year-old daughter, and at the age of twenty-six she had experienced her first full sensual pleasure. Her love for Matthew had achieved that, her complete love for everything about him.

'You sound surprised,' he gently teased.

Not even to Matthew could she admit, yet, the farce of her first marriage to Andrew. 'No, I——'

'I'm only teasing, darling.' He gave an exultant laugh. 'I want you again, Jessica.'

'I want you too,' she admitted shyly.

'I know,' he chuckled, suddenly serious as he began to kiss her.

Jessica felt that surging passion almost instantly this time, knew that she would never feel that restraint with Matthew again, that with him passion was a giving, not a taking.

She woke slowly the next morning, wrapped in a beautiful lethargy, wonderfully satiated. The night she had just spent in Matthew's arms had been beyond anything she had ever thought possible.

'Wake up, sleepyhead,' he murmured against her throat, his voice sounding lazily satisfied.

'Mm.' She stretched languidly, a dreamy smile to her lips as she turned instinctively into his arms, her mouth open to his.

'I love you, Jessica,' he broke the kiss to groan.

'I love you too,' she answered without hesitation.

'I think we should go away on a honeymoon,' he said between kisses.

'But we've already had one,' she laughed a protest.

'Not like this one.' Matthew looked down at her wickedly, all his harshness gone, his expression relaxed and loving.

'Matthew! Penny could come in at any moment.'

'She won't.' His head lowered as his lips caressed her breast.

'Mummy, why—Oh!' Penny stood awkwardly in the open doorway. 'Mummy?' she said uncertainly.

Matthew collapsed against Jessica with a groan. 'But then again . . .' he muttered ruefully.

Jessica shot him a warning look, and sat up to hold out her hand to Penny. 'What is it, darling?'

Penny came slowly over to the bed, her eyes wide. 'I—Breakfast,' she said haltingly. 'You weren't downstairs like you usually are, so I—I thought maybe you weren't well.'

'Your mother is fine.' Matthew leant back against the headboard. 'And weren't you ever taught to knock on bedroom doors?' he reprimanded gently.

The little girl blushed, grimacing. 'I didn't—Mummy doesn't usually mind. And I never used to go into Daddy's bedroom, not after he was angry one day.'

Jessica saw Matthew's sudden interest, his narrow-eyed gaze moving from her back to Penny. 'Daddy's bedroom?' he prompted, making room for Penny on the bed with them.

She made herself comfortable between them. 'Daddy had the room next to Mummy's,' she revealed innocently. 'But this is so much nicer,' she grinned up at him.

'I think so,' he agreed softly.

Jessica slipped out of bed, studiously avoiding Matthew's intent gaze as she pulled on her robe. 'I'll get dressed,' she muttered.

'Jessica . . .'

She didn't turn. 'I have to get breakfast.' She escaped into the adjoining bathroom, leaning back against the door.

It had never occurred to her that Penny would reveal her sleeping arrangements with Andrew to Matthew. Until this morning Penny had never seen her in bed with Matthew, because as Penny said, she was usually in the kitchen by the time she came down for breakfast. But Matthew was going to ask some very probing questions about this.

She wasn't surprised to find him waiting for her when she came out of the bathroom, dressing awkwardly as he watched her.

'I sent Penny downstairs,' he finally spoke.

She nodded. 'She's hungry.'

'Jessica——'

'Not now, Matthew,' she pleaded. 'Let's talk about this later. I—There's too much to tell now.'

'When Penny's gone to bed?'

'Yes,' she agreed jerkily.

His arms went about her, their bodies moulded together. 'Do you still love me?'

'Oh yes,' she replied without hesitation.

He kissed her gently. 'That's all I need to know.'

'Do you love me?' she asked anxiously.

'For always. For ever,' he told her huskily. 'Nothing, and I mean nothing,' he repeated pointedly, 'will ever change that.'

She clung to him. 'I hope not.'

'Be sure,' his tawny gaze held her. 'You were always meant to be mine—and you'll stay mine.'

She carried his certainty with her all day, but nevertheless she was nervous of the time when Penny had gone to bed and Matthew demanded to be told everything. Because Matthew was the sort of man who wouldn't rest until he knew it all. And the way she knew she loved him she wanted to tell him it all, to share it with him. She only hoped he still loved her when she had told him.

He seemed in no hurry to press the matter once Penny had gone to bed, letting her get to the subject of Andrew in her own time.

'You want to know what Penny meant,' she said nervously at last, seated beside Matthew on the couch, his arm encouragingly about her shoulders.

'Only when you're ready to tell me,' he said softly.

She looked up at him, loving everything about him, the warmth of his eyes, the way his mouth quirked indulgently at the corners, his possessive hold. She couldn't lose his love now!

'Do you want to tell me?' he prompted at her silence.

'I——' she broke off as the doorbell rang.

'Who the hell can that be?' Matthew rasped at the

interruption, striding out to open the door.

Jessica leant weakly back on the couch. But when she saw who their visitor was her tension returned with a vengeance. Alicia Barry!

CHAPTER ELEVEN

'GOOD evening, Jessica,' Lisa drawled haughtily.

'Er—Hello.' She stood up, feeling awkward in her casual trousers and top. The other woman was looking very sophisticated in a royal blue coloured dress, her long legs thrust into high-heeled sandals.

'I'm sorry to interrupt your evening.' Her smile seemed to condradict her words. She turned to Matthew. 'I seem to have mislaid some notes, and I know you need them typed first thing in the morning. I wondered if they would be in your briefcase.'

He nodded. 'I'll have a look.'

'Thank you.'

Jessica eyed the other woman warily once they were alone, remembering all too vividly their last meeting.

Alicia obviously remembered it too. 'Did you wonder about Matthew and me while we were in London together?' Her mouth twisted mockingly.

'No.'

'You should have, Jessica,' she taunted, her beautiful head thrown back proudly. 'And you shouldn't have sent Matthew off after arguing with him.'

She paled, hating this woman—and knowing her hate was returned tenfold. 'Matthew didn't——'

'Didn't he?' she scorned.

'No,' she shook her head.

Lisa smiled, a smile without humour, one of malice. 'Oh, but he did, Jessica. He and I were lovers in London, and we'll be lovers here too.'

She remembered Matthew's gentleness last night, his

sincerity when he told her he loved her. 'I don't believe you,' she said confidently.

'Thank you, darling,' he said deeply as he walked into the room, his angry gaze now fixed on Alicia. 'What the hell do you think you're doing?' he rasped.

She looked unrepentant. 'I'm only telling your wife——'

'A pack of lies!' he finished grimly. 'We weren't lovers in London, we haven't been lovers for over two years.'

'Jessica doesn't believe that, do you, Jessica?' the other woman taunted.

'I—I—Yes,' Jessica said firmly.

Matthew pulled her to his side, his arm firm about her waist. 'I don't know what other lies Lisa's been telling you——'

'Only the truth, darling,' Lisa drawled.

'Be quiet!' he snapped savagely. 'I don't know why you're doing this, why you want to hurt Jessica by lying.'

'Oh, but Jessica knows,' she taunted. 'Don't you, Jessica?'

Jessica hung her head. 'Yes.'

'Well, I don't,' Matthew said harshly. 'And I don't need to. You're sacked, Lisa. Don't bother to come back to the office. I'll send anything on to you we find in your desk——'

Her mouth twisted. 'You're as damned supercilious as your wife——'

'Leave, Lisa,' he told her icily, 'before I throw you out.'

'Oh, I'm going,' she taunted. 'I'll leave you two to your sterile little marriage.'

'Why, you——'

'Hopeless, isn't she, Matthew?' Lisa scorned, taking great pleasure from the colour coming and fading in Jessica's cheeks. 'Andrew found her a complete wash-out.'

'Get out of here!' Matthew shouted, his eyes glittering dangerously.

'I told you, I'm going.' Her self-confidence hadn't slipped for a moment. 'I hope you'll be very happy together. There is just one thing, Matthew,' she paused deliberately, the tension in the room now so intense it could be physically felt. 'Maybe you should ask Jessica why she played the part of the grieving widow when she knew Andrew was divorcing her.' She walked to the door. 'I'll leave you two to have a pleasant evening. Goodnight.'

Jessica looked at Matthew once they were alone, seeing his stunned expression. Her heart sank. It looked as if Lisa's final thrust had done the trick. She was going to lose Matthew!

She put out a hand to him. 'Matthew——'

'Is it true?' he said expressionlessly. 'Was he going to divorce you?'

She gripped her hands together. 'Yes.'

'Why?'

'To marry Alicia.'

Matthew's breath caught in his throat. 'Did you love him?'

'No.'

'No?' he repeated incredulously.

Jessica closed her eyes, taking a controlling breath. 'I was eighteen when I married him, and I thought I loved him. It was only—later that I realised I didn't.'

'Later?' he prompted harshly.

'There were other women, always other women. Lisa was far from being the first.'

'But he had decided to marry her?'

'Yes.'

'He'd already told you he wanted a divorce?'

She nodded. 'The night of the accident.'

'My God!' Matthew sank down into a chair. 'I

thought you loved him. I thought he was the reason I couldn't get near you, why you would never give yourself to me as you did last night.'

Jessica went down on her knees beside the chair he sat in. 'You have to know how it was between Andrew and me, Matthew, not just parts of it,' she held his hands in hers, her gaze pleading on his pale face.

'Then tell it to me,' he said dully.

It was hard to talk at first, to tell him things she had never told anyone else, all the bad memories locked up inside her that had held her a prisoner for so long. She told him of the challenge she had been to Andrew, of their wedding night, of the nights after that when he had abused her, of his violent tempers, the temper he had had that last Christmas, his taunts when she had refused to share his bed just after Penny was born. Matthew listened incredulously at first, and then angrily, his face darkening with fury.

'The bastard!' He stood forcefully to his feet, his hands clenching and unclenching.

Jessica felt spent, her emotions raw, needing his comfort more than his anger, although she knew his anger wasn't directed at her but at Andrew. For now. But she still had more to tell him.

'Why didn't you leave him?' he demanded to know. 'You didn't love him, so why didn't you divorce him?'

She licked suddenly dry lips. 'There was Penny——'

'Penny was frightened of him,' he dismissed. 'That's become obvious the three months we've been married.'

She knew he was right. She had thought Penny's nightmares were caused because of Andrew's absence, now she believed it was the thought that he might suddenly return that worried Penny the most. She had had no idea that Penny was so affected by her father's cruelty, but Matthew's gentleness with her had proved that she was.

'I was his wife——'

'And you hated him.' Matthew's eyes narrowed on her bowed head. 'You hadn't slept with him for over five years. I find this so hard to believe,' he shook his head. 'We all thought you loved him—Peg, George, *me.*' He sighed. 'I thought that was the reason you put up with his other women. Why did you put up with his behaviour, Jessica?'

She turned away. 'We were married, and I didn't take my marriage vows lightly.' Now that it had come to the moment of truth she couldn't tell him, couldn't tell him that last final secret that had kept her Andrew's captive.

'Why the hell did you take them at all?' Matthew rasped. 'You were never meant to be his wife, Jessica. The night I met you, I looked up and saw your reflection in the window, and I thought I was dreaming. You were everything I ever wanted, all my fantasies in one woman. When I realised you were real I knew I couldn't let you escape, that you were the woman who had been created for me, just as I was the man who had been created for you. To find that you hadn't waited for our meeting, as I had, that you already had a husband, nearly killed me.'

She remembered his cryptic comment the first night they had met about how he had been patient and waited for her, knowing he told the truth about loving her even then, that everything he had said and done since then had been because he loved her.

'I was young, and suddenly alone. I needed someone to love me,' she defended. 'I—I thought Andrew did. By the time I realised he didn't it was already too late.'

'But later—later you could have divorced him.'

'No,' she choked.

'Why the hell not?'

She breathed hard, her eyes wild as she stood up, the final moment of truth upon her. 'Because he would have taken Penny from me! He would have taken the one thing I had to love,' she finished brokenly, her shoulders shaking as she cried.

'He couldn't have——'

'Yes, he could,' she told him fiercely.

Matthew frowned, his gaze searching. 'What haven't you told me, Jessica?' He came forward to grasp her shoulders. 'What are you keeping from me?'

She couldn't look at his face, staring woodenly at one of the buttons on his shirt. 'I had a nervous breakdown,' she revealed in a dull voice. 'Andrew was going to claim that I was mentally unstable so that he could have custody of Penny if I ever divorced him. I would have taken any amount of his abuse to keep Penny. I've even offered to resume sleeping with him to stop him leaving me.'

She felt Matthew flinch. 'Did he ever accept?'

'No,' she gave a bitter laugh. 'Didn't you hear Alicia—I'm a wash-out. Or at least, I was,' she blushed.

'What does that mean?' he frowned.

'Last night,' she wetted her lips nervously, 'when you and I—When we——'

His hands tightened painfully on her arms. 'You've never known physical pleasure before,' he said in a stunned voice. 'Is that it, Jessica? He never gave you that pleasure?'

She leant weakly against him. 'Never,' she told him huskily.

'I didn't realise——! I thought when you said your wedding night had been a failure that you'd worked things out later. I didn't know... ' Matthew shook his head dazedly.

'Andrew said I was frigid, that I was no good in bed. When I—when I said that maybe it was partly his fault he said that no other woman he had slept with had the same trouble, that there was something wrong with me.'

'And you believe him?' Matthew said angrily. 'If I'd only known!' he groaned. 'There's never been anything wrong with you, Jessica, except the inadequacies he forced on you. By telling you you were no good he brainwashed you into believing it.' He gently touched her cheek. 'When I made love to you and you were cold towards me I thought it was because you were in love with the way he'd made love to you, that I was failing you. And all the time he'd convinced you that you couldn't feel physical pleasure,' he ground out. 'Love is all you need, my darling, love that I intend to give you the rest of our lives. Now tell me about the breakdown,' he probed gently.

Jessica stiffened. 'Andrew said I was mentally unstable——'

'Andrew didn't know what he was talking about,' he denied harshly. 'If that were the case you would have collapsed when he died and left you all those debts. Instead you got your life together, went out to work, and paid up all the money he owed.'

'Except to you.'

His expression softened. 'Consider it paid in full. So why the breakdown, Jessica?'

She bit her top lip, breathing heavily. 'I found out—Andrew wasn't with me when Penny was born. I thought he was working, and being a salesman it wasn't always easy to reach him. I found out later that he was with another woman.'

'How?'

'She came to see me two months after Penny was born. She—she said she was pregnant herself, but that Andrew refused to acknowledge that the child was his. I—I just collapsed, went to pieces. They took me into hospital for a while, and then sent me home. But I never let Andrew near me again. I couldn't—couldn't bear for him to touch me. When I asked him later about the girl he said she'd had an abortion.' She shivered. 'After that, whenever I threatened to end the marriage Andrew always said he would take Penny from me.'

Matthew shook his head. 'No court would have given him custody of Penny.'

'But my breakdown——'

'Have you heard of post-natal depression?'

'They mentioned it at the hospital, but I didn't understand what they meant.'

'Well, I don't know too much about it myself,' he admitted ruefully. 'I think it's something to do with the hormonal changes in the body after giving birth. I think that's what you were suffering from. You couldn't possibly be expected to cope with that, a baby, and the misery Andrew put you through.'

Hope lightened her expression. 'Do you really think that's true?'

'I'm sure that's what they were trying to tell you at the hospital,' he nodded, his arms coming about her. 'Now suppose we go upstairs and prove just how frigid you *aren't*?'

After the intensity of the last few minutes his teasing was welcome. 'You still love me?'

'More than ever,' he nodded. 'Did you think I wouldn't?'

'I don't know,' she clung to him. 'I love you so much, I couldn't bear to lose you.'

'You're my other half, Jessica, to leave you now would be like ripping my heart out. And I've never had masochistic tendancies,' he added lightly. 'I love you, darling,' he said seriously. 'And that means for a lifetime.'

Jessica hummed happily to herself as she drove home. Dr Harper had given her some happy news, and she could hardly wait to tell Matthew.

'Darling——'

'Thank God you're home!' He grabbed hold of her arm as soon as she entered the house, dragging her towards the lounge.

'What is it?' she asked sharply. 'Jeremy . . .?'

Matthew looked very harassed, not at all the competent businessman he was. 'He's upset, and I can't seem to calm him down. Penny tried too, but he wants you.'

The lounge looked as if it had been hit by a whirlwind, toys everywhere, her twelve-week-old son lying angelically in his cot, gurgling happily as his indulgent older sister played with his rattle, Penny totally enchanted with this new member of the family.

Jessica turned to look at a rather sheepish Matthew, her love glowing in her eyes. It was just over a year since the night she had told Matthew everything about her past life, and it had been a year of discovery, of being cossetted with so much love that she often felt like a contented cat. Three months ago she had given Matthew a son, had watched the pride and joy on his face as Jeremy made his entrance into the world.

Matthew often changed and played with their son, but her visit to the doctor today had been the first time she had left him solely in charge of the baby. It obviously hadn't been a complete success.

'Well, he *was* upset,' Matthew mumbled ruefully.

'Of course he was, darling.' She kissed him lovingly on the mouth before going into the kitchen to unpack her shopping.

Matthew's eyes widened as he followed her into the kitchen, looking suspiciously at the food. 'Steak,' he said slowly, watching as she took out the peppers and mushrooms she was going to use for the sauce, 'Champagne?' His suspicion grew as she put the bottle in the refrigerator.

'What's the matter, darling?' She eyed him teasingly.

'The last time you gave me champagne you told me you were expecting Jeremy.'

'Well, it can't be that this time,' she smiled.

'No,' he grimaced. 'What did Dr Harper have to say?' he asked hopefully.

Her eyes glowed with love as she moved into his arms. 'She says I'm very healthy.'

'And?' he prompted.

Her mouth quirked. 'And that I can make love to my husband any time I want to.'

Desire flared in the depths of his tawny eyes, his arms tightened convulsively about her. 'She did?' he groaned.

'Yes,' Jessica gave a happy laugh.

'Now?' Matthew said urgently.

'Penny and Jeremy,' she reminded him with a contented giggle.

'Yes,' he moaned. 'But I've been in agony for weeks now, lying beside you and unable to do more than hold you, I suppose I can wait another few hours.'

'It will be worth it, darling,' she said huskily.

'With you it always is,' and his mouth claimed her, promising her a passion that would last a lifetime.

Harlequin® Plus

THE ORIGIN OF THE TEDDY BEAR

In *Captive Loving,* Jessica's little daughter, Penny, has a very bedraggled but much-loved teddy bear, which accompanies her everywhere. This famous children's toy, part of the childhood memories of many, has fairly recent origins.

In 1902, the president of the United States, Theodore "Teddy" Roosevelt, went to Mississippi and Louisiana to settle a border dispute by "drawing the line" between the two states. Roosevelt loved bear hunting, and a famous newspaper cartoonist named Clifford Berryman drew a cartoon of the president holding a gun and refusing to shoot a small bear cub. Berryman entitled the cartoon "Drawing the line in Mississippi," and it appeared in newspapers and magazines across the country.

In Brooklyn, New York, a Russian immigrant named Morris Michtom owned a candy store, where he and his wife sold small toys they made by hand. When they saw the cartoon with the cute little bear cub, they determined then and there to make a toy bear. The first bear was made of brown felt with movable limbs and button eyes. It was placed in the window with a copy of the famous cartoon and a sign saying "Teddy's Bear." It was immediately sold, and the Michtoms' customers clamored for more. But, hesitant to continue using the president's name, Michtom wrote to Mr. Roosevelt for permission, enclosing one of his stuffed bears. The president replied saying the Michtoms were welcome to use it. The teddy bear was born!

This cuddly toy quickly became enormously popular in England and Europe, as well as in America. Today, teddy bears are still as much a part of childhood as Santa Claus and the Easter Bunny.

The fate of the original bear the Michtoms sent to President Roosevelt? He now resides in honor in Washington, D.C.'s famous Smithsonian Institution.